THE MOON GLOW BOOKSHOP

THE MOON GLOW BOOKSHOP

Dongwon Seo

Translated from the Korean
by Shanna Tan

Copyright © Dongwon Seo 2022
English translation © Shanna Tan 2025

The right of Dongwon Seo to be identified as the Author
of the Work has been asserted by him in accordance
with the Copyright, Designs and Patents Act 1988.

Originally published in South Korea as 달 드링크 서점
by Moohak Soochup Publishing Co. Ltd in 2022.

First published in hardback in 2025 by Wildfire
An imprint of Headline Publishing Group Limited,
in arrangement with Moohak Soochup Publishing Co. Ltd,
BC Agency and Mulcahy Sweeney Literary Agency.

1

Apart from any use permitted under UK copyright law, this publication may
only be reproduced, stored, or transmitted, in any form, or by any means,
with prior permission in writing of the publishers or, in the case of
reprographic production, in accordance with the terms of licences
issued by the Copyright Licensing Agency.

Rabbit illustrations © FreePik/Amahce

All characters in this publication are fictitious and any resemblance
to real persons, living or dead, is purely coincidental.

Cataloguing in Publication Data is available from the British Library

Hardback ISBN 978 1 0354 2544 0
Trade Paperback ISBN 978 1 0354 2543 3

Typeset in 12.1/15.95pt Bembo MT Pro by Six Red Marbles UK, Thetford, Norfolk

Printed and bound in Great Britain by Clays Ltd, Elcograf S.p.A.

Headline's policy is to use papers that are natural, renewable and recyclable
products and made from wood grown in well-managed forests and other
controlled sources. The logging and manufacturing processes are expected
to conform to the environmental regulations of the country of origin.

Headline Publishing Group Limited
An Hachette UK Company
Carmelite House
50 Victoria Embankment
London EC4Y 0DZ

The authorised representative in the EEA is Hachette Ireland,
8 Castlecourt Centre, Dublin 15, D15 XTP3, Ireland (email: info@hbgi.ie)

www.headline.co.uk
www.hachette.co.uk

THE MOON GLOW BOOKSHOP

Prologue

Sometimes, it was a hidden spot in a busy building; other times, it blended into the serene landscape. Occasionally, it stood alone, like a café next to the park.

Right now, here it was.

'I'm telling you; I came from the moon. Did you hear me? Nobody understands me.'

Slumped on the table was a woman, clearly drunk. The alcohol must've gotten to her for she wasn't making sense at all.

'Assholes. Horrible humans! Don't give me that crap about *That's how society works*. Freeze to death, y'all!'

Usual drunken drivel.

Often, it was the polite ones, those with a smile perpetually plastered on their faces, who had the thickest layer of dust covering their hearts. The type who masked their feelings behind a concrete wall. This woman was one such person.

'Puuu—'

She expelled a deep sigh, and on top of her head, a pair of long bunny ears flopped.

'I worked so damn hard!'

The next moment, she crumbled into tears. Piecing together her drunken spiel, one could glean she must've been fired from her job. In the empty shop, her only companion was the bartender behind the counter.

Throughout her rant, he'd been listening in silence. His hair was a striking blue and on his chest was a name tag – *MUN*.

'I believe you.'

The bartender, who'd not moved a single inch, had suddenly spoken. But his next words were completely unexpected.

'That you came from the moon, and that you're a strong rabbit.'

Did I say I was a strong rabbit?

The woman lifted her head, which felt several times heavier than usual, and stared at the man.

Thud—

He placed something on the table. A name tag resembling the same design as his own.

'Would you like to work here?'

Huh? Who offers a job to a stranger they've just met? Her sluggish brain struggled to understand what was going on. But she had no intention of rejecting this sudden proposal. She was that desperate.

'Yes! I'm a good worker. Leave all the physical work to me.'

She nodded vigorously, looking up at him with round, eager eyes. Wait, did he already know that she would come? The name tag on the table spelt out the words: *MOON RABBIT*.

Chapter 1

If Your Life Were a Book

'I'm a fool.'

Dressed in a sharp suit, the man's outfit was rather at odds with the stubble that dotted his chin and his long hair pulled back into a ponytail. Dae-il was in a particularly foul mood today. He always had a piercing gaze, but right now, his expression could cut through glass.

If I knew this was a bar, I wouldn't have stepped in!

Like on any other day, Dae-il only left his art studio in the wee hours. The only difference was, today, he'd discovered a new shop tucked away in a deserted alley.

Normally, he would have walked past without much thought, perhaps muttering under his breath that a shop in the middle of nowhere would go bust in no time. However, what made him turn his head once more was the writing on the sign.

IF YOUR LIFE WERE A BOOK

These days, provocative and sensationalised messages were everywhere, hence it'd been a long while since he'd come across a line so soothing and nostalgic. Upon closer inspection, the shop exterior bore an uncanny resemblance to the bookshop he used to frequent as a kid.

Ah, how he used to stand next to the shelves and devour a book in one sitting! Even though he never purchased anything, the old lady who owned the place always welcomed him heartily. At this thought, a warmth spread in his chest, thawing the stiffness in his posture. He slowly looked up and was greeted by a sign that seemed far too big for the tiny shopfront.

THE MOON GLOW BOOKSHOP

What was that common saying? *Nothing sells better than nostalgia.* Indeed. Swept up in the sentimentality of the moment, Dae-il found himself pushing the door open and stepping inside.

'Can I get you a story?'

The waitress approached softly, clutching a menu. Her name tag read MOON RABBIT. He glanced up. On top of her head sat a pair of droopy bunny ears.

He shook his head.

Guess this place is no different.

Waitresses wearing bunny ears; a drinking spot masquerading as a bookshop. In the end, it was one of the many gimmicky traps out there making bankroll on nostalgia by luring customers in.

When did the world start to become like instant food? These days, everything was about speed, spiciness, the umami factor or whatever it was. When the mass media started touting wellness trends, Dae-il couldn't help but snort in derision at the ostentatiousness of it all.

In the end, what brought in the money were things that tantalised the tastebuds and piled on the fats. And he wasn't just thinking about food.

Park Dae-il. When introducing himself, Dae-il preferred using the title 'artist', not 'painter'. At least, the version of himself in the past did.

How beautiful.

There was a time once when he had stood in front of a painting, tears running down his face. He yearned to create a work like that, a painting that would comfort the person looking at it. To Dae-il, only a true work of art could elicit such a reaction, a story within the frame.

He was reasonably talented. When he closed his eyes, emotions would surge, and he'd submit himself to the slight buzz running through his nerves, an outpouring of feelings that guided his hands to glide across the canvas, and when he next emerged from this zone, a painting would be completed.

However, that was a long, long time ago.

One day, the gallery manager spoke to him, his brows knitted in a crease.

'Dae-il, such stuff no longer sells.'

Dae-il was struck speechless. He painted in the hope of bringing comfort to others. Even if nobody wanted to buy them, he was proud of his creations. And if his paintings could evoke the same sense of nostalgia in others as they did in himself, he'd consider that an accomplishment. It was what drew him to art in the first place, and why he would even pay out of his own pocket to take part in art exhibitions. But this meant that as time passed, he was finding it increasingly harder to make ends meet.

I was wrong.

When he could no longer afford even the cheapest of necessities, Dae-il finally bowed down to reality. He started painting stuff that brought in the bread.

A Skeleton in a Perfectionist's Closet
An Insomniac Blonde Femme Fatale
A Madman's Pleasure
A Swooning Heart of Illicit Affairs

Works that attracted the eyeballs at the first glance. Electrifying, sensational. But like a dynamite bomb, after the first explosion that overpowers the senses, only a desolate emptiness remained.

'Wisdom', 'comfort' – words that were apparently out of vogue. Dae-il struggled to suppress the disgust welling up from deep within him.

How dare they call themselves stories?

It was as though a giant, rough hand had seized him by the scruff of the neck and flung him into a ravine of darkness.

Right now, he was experiencing that same rotten feeling again.

Even a bar has the nerve to call their drinks 'stories'?

He glared at the menu in disdain.

'In this section of the menu, we have a selection of stories set in the Wild West, and here are ones with the universe as a backdrop. And stories about other planets are right here.'

The bunny-eared waitress pointed them out in the menu as she spoke. Was this all because they have chosen 'a bookshop' as a concept? The atmosphere in here didn't feel *that* offensive, not even the bunny ears.

It wasn't as if the lady was in a bunny costume, nor was her face painted with thick eyeliner or bright red lipstick. She had a fresh, simple vibe about her, and her long, unpermed hair reminded him of a conscientious granddaughter working at a bookshop owned by her grandmother.

'How uncanny – neither here nor there.'

'Excuse me?'

Flustered that he'd unwittingly blurted out this thought, he quickly covered it up by pointing at a random item on the menu.

'Ah. *The Boy Who Sees*. Shall I get you this one?'

He nodded in reply and the staff member with the bunny ears crinkled her eyes up in a polite smile before heading back towards the counter.

Me and my big mouth.

Dae-il had deliberately chosen a spot where he wouldn't have to face a bartender. He had no wish to make any amount of small talk with a stranger. For him, the only way to converse with people was through paintings.

That said, he enjoyed visiting new places. Being in a different environment gave him inspiration. Life had been exhausting, and it'd been a long while since he'd had the luxury to sit down and observe his surroundings. And this place had great ambience, he admitted. Soaking in the atmosphere, he slowly relaxed.

How did I not notice this place before?

He was captivated by the soft glow of the lights in the dimly lit bar. With its dark wood furnishings, the shop reminded him of a library.

Well, the only flaw is the rows of vari-coloured bottles of spirits where books should be.

Because he was the only customer, Dae-il felt more at ease than he had for a long time. Was there ever a place besides his studio that made him feel so comfortable? In fact, he might even like it better here, considering how he had been forced to paint art that didn't square with him.

For a moment, Dae-il let himself be carried by the flow of time. *Tick-tock, tick-tock.* The second hand on the wall clock felt as though it was slowing down. A wave of exhaustion washed over him. His eyelids grew heavy, as if he could doze off at any moment. *Am I already in a dream?* he wondered, as his consciousness faded out.

Tak—!

A loud thud made him jerk upright. *Shrupp*, he sucked in his saliva and whipped his head around. He swore he heard the sound right next to his ear, but there was nobody near him.

'Your story is ready.' A lilting voice spoke. It was the bartender with the striking blue hair standing behind the counter. In front of him was a tall, cylindrical glass.

'Uh hm.'

Hoping to conceal the fact that he'd dozed off, Dae-il deliberately made a show of rising from his seat and drawing himself upright as he walked towards the bar. He pulled out the chair in front of his drink, smoothed the creases in his suit, and sat down slowly at the counter. He was pleased with himself, with how he feigned casualness. But as soon as he reached for the glass, a thought hit him.

I should have waited to be served.

If he'd remained in his seat, surely the server would have brought his drink to him. His pride took a hit. *So much for wanting to keep a dignified appearance*, he thought. You might be questioning his obsession with etiquette in a bar, but this was of the utmost importance to Dae-il. Thinking that he might as well go all the way to keep up with the pretence, he acted as if he'd intended to chat with the bartender.

'A cosy shop you have here,' Dae-il commented as he lifted

the glass. Was he nervous? He detected a rough edge in his own voice.

'Thank you,' the bartender replied smoothly.

Dae-il was relieved. It seemed like the bartender hadn't caught on to his awkwardness. He glanced at the man's name tag – *MUN*.

'Looks like business is slow?'

Oh shit. How rude to point out the obvious. It was always like this with Dae-il. He couldn't seem to stop himself from saying things that made the other person uncomfortable. Even when he became belatedly conscious of his callousness, he would continue to run his mouth. When he tried to salvage the situation, his mind would draw a blank. If an idea ever came to him, it was probably too late; he would already be lying in bed at night.

His lack of filter, together with his stand-offish vibes, made him unpopular. Back in school, his only friends were books and paintings.

Mun smiled lightly. 'Yeah, we don't get many customers.'

Dae-il wondered if being a bartender meant he was used to dealing with all types of people. He couldn't detect any trace of discomfort on the man's face.

'The upside is that we get to have a good chat with every customer.'

The bartender's friendliness made Dae-il uncomfortable. He was not used to being treated like a friend by a stranger. His lips trembled and went rogue again. 'If you do business this way, you'll be in for a hard time. No matter how much you enjoy the work, if you can't make a living from it, everything will crumble.'

His eyes flashed, as they did whenever he tried to conceal

his fluster. *Dae-il, stop talking!* Even as he screamed internally, he continued to blabber on.

'Of course, if the drinks are good, then that's a different story.'

Wait. He was supposed to take a sip first and say, 'Ah, but the drinks are great, so I'm sure business will pick up very soon.' However, the words had rolled out before his lips had even touched the glass. The worst thing was, he'd sounded like a pretentious food critic when he wasn't even a good drinker. This was a complete disaster.

'Take your time and enjoy the drink.'

The bartender continued to smile affably. While Dae-il's expression remained sharp, inwardly he was dying of embarrassment. He decided he would knock back the drink and quickly make his way out.

Raising his glass, Dae-il wondered if he should just close his eyes and empty it in one gulp. He hated the smell of alcohol. However, when he peered at the drink, he changed his mind.

'What is this?'

The cocktail was divided into layers, each of a different colour, as though it held a rainbow within. Dae-il shook the glass slightly, but the colours didn't mix. He was mesmerised.

'It's what you ordered – *The Boy Who Sees*. Best savoured layer by layer.'

It was a beautiful cocktail. Even Dae-il, who wasn't fond of alcohol, was captivated by the shimmering layers. It was as if colourful lights were swirling within. This could be good enough to be called a story. Dae-il was satisfied with his choice.

'Looks delicious.'

It was almost too beautiful to drink. The top layer shone a brilliant emerald green. His attention was held by the glimmer. *I'm glad I came in*, he thought as he carefully tilted the glass towards his lips and took a sip.

Ew, what the hell is this?

All his earlier musings, waxing lyrical about the beautiful drink, were overturned at the first sip. Bitterness and a nausea-inducing smell attacked his senses. If he didn't know better, he'd have thought he just drank sewage water. Just as he was about to spit it out, a vision intruded into his mind.

A child was born. The child had strong legs and when he was older, he grew to like football. No, he *loved* football. Sweat dripped down his temples, and as he steadied his heavy breathing, he told himself, *I can do this.* He aimed a kick, and he scored, crowning him the hero on the field. He would never forget the moment he was scouted to join the Youth World Cup.

However, without warning, his world came crashing down. On the morning of the competition, he woke up late. Having missed the bus to the stadium, he ended up taking a taxi with his mother. Throughout the ride, he couldn't stop blaming her for not waking him up. The tantrums of an immature child. Who would have thought it would be their last moments together?

It was a car accident. Something that could have happened anywhere, to anyone. This time, it overturned the taxi the boy and his mother were in. Luckily, his strong legs escaped unscathed. But his mother, who wrapped the boy protectively in her arms, died. The misfortune didn't end there. A shard of glass stabbed the boy in his eye. It was unfortunate. The boy was robbed of the light in his bright eyes. Blinded, he could no longer play football, and his childhood dream shattered.

'Argh. Ugh.'

The oppressive despair wracking Dae-il's body slowly dissipated. His throat was burning. He'd swallowed the drink without meaning to. A fire welled up in him as he glared daggers at the bartender.

'What the hell did you spike that drink with?'

'An infusion of a boy's story.'

The man's expression remained calm, and this only fuelled Dae-il's anger.

What the fuck did he give me?

To Dae-il, a painting was like a story because it would call up different memories for different people looking at it. But he hadn't expected the sensation of having a hallucination or augmented reality of some kind forced upon him.

Was it drugs?

Hands trembling, he looked wildly around the shop. His thirst was intensifying with each second. He was going to die. He was desperate for anything that could douse the fiery thirst.

'Water! Give me water!'

'If you need a drink, there's one right in front of you.'

If not for his burning throat, Dae-il would have screamed. Was this the bartender's revenge for criticising his shop? But the drink was served before their awkward conversation.

Dae-il's imagination began to run wild. Was the bartender a psychotic murderer? Taking advantage of an empty shop to poison the next unfortunate soul that wandered in?

'I-I beg you!'

If he wasn't given something right now, he would surely die. Was this humility in the face of death? His rage withered into fear. The only person who could save him was the man in front of him.

'The second layer will be an easier drink.'

The bartender pointed at the glass. The emerald layer was gone, revealing the gleam of crimson beneath. An ominous glow.

'Water . . .'

He'd reached his limits. It was as if his nostrils were stuffed with the hottest red pepper. Losing his grip on logic, he set his eyes on the drink once more.

It's a different colour. Maybe I'll be fine.

Desperation drove him to reach out for the glass.

'Ah.'

It was like swallowing whole strawberries blended in milk. The pain slowly subsided. Along with the sense of relief enveloping his body, another scene flitted into his mind.

Over time, the deep wounds began to heal. He eased into a new routine. However, his sight would never return, just like how desolation would never leave him. Depression and an overwhelming sense of helplessness weighed down on him. The boy's father tried tirelessly to save his son. Perhaps the boy sensed his father's efforts, for he slowly learned to cope with the sadness. His father wasn't the only one who fought hard for him.

He had a childhood friend. Unlike the others who gradually drifted away from him, she was always by his side.

After the incident, the boy became sensitive and irritable, and it wasn't easy for people around him. However, there was something that melted a corner of his walled-up heart – the piano.

His childhood friend was good at the piano. For a long time, the boy simply listened to her play, but one day, he asked, 'Can I try?' The girl nodded, and seeing the effort she put in to teach and to care for him, one could almost forget that she was still a child herself.

Time passed, and they were now high school students. Over the years, he'd become the better pianist.

'Haa—' The wracking coughs subsided. But the pain had tears pooling at the corners of his eyes.

'You.' Dae-il's glare sharpened. His grim mood contorted his harsh features.

'That was sweet, right?' The bartender grinned in delight. In the face of such pure joy, it was almost embarrassing to think about flying into a rage. True to the bartender's words, the crimson layer was like honey. It soothed his pain and misery, and a lingering scent permeated his senses long after he'd swallowed. The aroma was so intoxicating that Dae-il couldn't bear to let go of the glass.

'I'm warning you, if you're feeding me something strange . . . I mean . . .'

He couldn't string a sentence together. A flush shooting up from his ears to his forehead told him he was getting tipsy.

Instead of speaking, he tried to convey his warning in his stare. There were times, he knew, that his fierce glare could be put to good use.

'Alcohol is such a strange thing, isn't it?'

The bartender didn't appear cowed at all. He continued smiling, tossing out light jokes. Meanwhile, Dae-il was starting to get confused about why he was angry.

What the bartender said was true. With so many types of

liquor out there, there were bound to be some that would burn the throat. It would have been nice if he'd been given a warning, but he couldn't quite complain about it. After all, he was the one who had chosen the drink; all the bartender did was make his order.

'Ahem.' Embarrassed by his outburst, Dae-il cleared his throat. 'The alcohol must have gotten to me. Please excuse me.'

'The first sip always hits the hardest. Here. Have a small bite to go with your drink. It's on the house.'

On the round plate were cherry tomatoes sliced into halves. Complete with fresh salad leaves and dressing, it looked like a nicely plated side dish from a fine-dining restaurant. At that thought, he remembered his woefully thin wallet.

'I must tell you first. I don't have much money.'

'Don't worry. We have more than enough food to serve you something. Our fridge is bursting.'

At the bartender's light-hearted tone, a weight seemed to be lifted from his heart.

'You're good to your customers. So, well, I'm sure this place will become famous soon.'

Finally, his words had come out right.

Using a small fork, Dae-il stabbed at a tiny tomato and put it into his mouth.

'Does this dish have a name?'

'Of course. It's called "The Tomatoes That Want to Open Up". Those who eat it will feel compelled to share more about themselves.'

Dae-il chuckled softly. Serving a nice snack on the house was probably the bar's strategy to get more regular customers, but somehow, it felt like the man was truly interested to hear his story.

'No free lunch in the world, eh?'

'You could say that.'

Dae-il didn't like opening up to others. But somehow, today, he felt like it would be okay to do so.

'I paint for a living. But what I do is a far cry from art. It's just stuff that can sell. Paintings that are provocative, sensual. The times of valuing precious memories are long gone. I tried my best to stick to my style, but everyone tells me to paint things that are more sensational, more visceral. Sometimes, when I'm forced to work with nude models, I find myself wondering what I am doing with my life.'

Dae-il pierced a couple of tomato halves with the fork and ate them. He resented how negativity surrounded him all the time.

'I am a failure. I abandoned my dreams a long time ago.'

Dae-il was gloomy. The bitter aftertaste in his mouth refused to be washed away no matter how many tomatoes he ate. Because he knew he would spout a peevish comment each time he opened his mouth, Dae-il became reluctant to share his feelings. He was like a jar of rotten fish. Opening it would only release a hideous stench, and nothing good would come out of it.

'You're pretty cool for someone who claims to have failed.'

It seemed like the bartender was trying to lighten the mood. He cast his eyes over Dae-il's clean-cut suit.

'Oh. This. There's a story behind it.'

'What's the story?'

'Well . . . nothing amazing.'

'Would you like more tomatoes?'

'You're a mischievous one.'

Dae-il let out a sigh. But the corner of his lips lifted slightly. He was thankful that the bartender remained cheery even as he listened to his story.

'There's someone I love dearly. In the past, that person once told me he was embarrassed by me.'

'Oh, I'm sorry to hear that.'

'No, it's fine. I can see what he meant. I used to dress shabbily. So, after that day, I started paying more attention to my appearance. And my manners and etiquette. Everyone found the new me better, so that was probably a good change. But everything crumbles once I let myself go for a second.' Rubbing the stubble on his chin, Dae-il chuckled.

'I'm envious. I can barely grow any facial hair.'

Dae-il scrutinised the bartender's face. He looked rather young to own a bar. *Probably in his mid-twenties, or younger,* Dae-il thought.

'Well, in any case. Unlike you, who is already a boss at your age, I'm in my mid-fifies but have yet to achieve my dreams.'

The bartender checked his watch. Suddenly, Dae-il was struck with a thought. *Am I in my fifties already?* He quickly shook it off. *Must be feeling a little out of it because I haven't had a drink in a long time.*

'Shall we live vicariously then?' The bartender glanced at Dae-il's hand, or rather, the glass in it. 'The next layer is even sweeter.'

'Looks a little thin this time.'

'The best moments are the shortest.'

There were only two layers left. Unlike the last layer, which took up a third of the glass, the next layer was barely a mouthful.

It was so good just now. How much sweeter can this get?
Feeling excited, he tipped the glass.
'Mmm—'
It was like inhaling clouds. The bubbles fizzled in his mouth, lifting his mood. As the liquid glided down his throat, a lovely scent swirled in his palate, tickling the tip of his nose, lifting the corner of his lips.

Having lost his sight, the boy couldn't even make out the objects in front of him. However, he felt the tiny tingles in his fingertips more vividly than anyone else.

The vibrations as he pressed down on a key. The subtle differences depending on the surroundings. He loved how the reverberations sometimes came together in a crescendo, while other times they faded out, *al niente*. He saw things he hadn't seen with his eyes, and realised in that moment, that the most precious of things may not be visible.

As for his childhood friend, the two of them remained as close even as the boy turned into a young man. He felt the indescribable warmth enveloping him and knew this was yet another of those things that even a sighted person might not see. He proposed to the girl, who'd turned into a young woman, and with a tinkle of a laugh, she said yes.

By then, the young man's talents had blossomed. Everyone adored the music he made, and he became a pianist whose talents were unrivalled.

'Can I have one more glass of this, please?'
Drunk in the moment of ecstasy, Dae-il couldn't hide his disappointment as the vision faded out.

'If you would like another drink, you'll have to empty the glass first.'

'Happy to.'

'Mr Park Dae-il.' Just as he was about to down the last of the drink, the bartender called his name. The frosty undertone in the man's voice made Dae-il's hand stop mild-tilt.

'It'll be a bitter ending. Whatever you have experienced in the first mouthful will be nothing compared to this.'

'Isn't it normal for alcohol to be bitter? The middle bits aren't alcohol, right? Anyway, for my next drink, I would like a whole glass of the blue liquid in the earlier layer.'

'That, too, is alcohol. We must take care not to overindulge.'

Dae-il wasn't paying attention. His face flushed red from the alcohol.

'A few drinks aren't going to kill me, are they? I'll finish this in a second, so please start preparing my next drink.'

Gulp, gulp. He poured the rest of the cocktail into his mouth and shook the empty glass above his head – a sign that he was done.

'See? This is nothin—'

The next moment, it was as if someone had taken a club to his head. He realised his horrible mistake. However, it was too late. He'd let the bartender's advice fall on deaf ears and emptied the glass.

He screamed.

Sharp pain coursed through his body, and he felt his consciousness slipping away. His hands were trembling uncontrollably.

'W-what's happening?'

The young man was always No. 1. However, with passing time, the title of 'the best' felt like a choker around his neck. The scrutiny of the public had long since turned to pressure, and because of his sudden slump, it was as if he was *this* close to relinquishing the position he'd held for such a long time to his competitors.

He was upset. Nobody else knew what true music was. Only he, who didn't rely on sight, but submitted himself to the reverberations of the notes, was the real deal. Plagued by such thoughts, his performances only worsened. As the love showered upon him swerved into indifference, the vibrations on his fingertips that had revived his heartbeat disappeared. As for his lover, he no longer cared for her. He cared more about getting back the public's attention.

Eventually, he went down the route that he should never have taken. He'd heard rumours that there were drugs that would help him make music that was out of this world. He had the money, and there was no shortage of people who were eyeing his wealth. Getting his hands on the substances was a breeze.

His lover tried to stop him. But he was no longer the person she recognised. She grew to tiptoe around him, especially if there were items within his reach. When he had one of his tantrums, everything around him could be reduced to broken shards on the ground.

Perhaps the rumours were true, for his music once again captivated the masses. He was not afraid of the police. He could count on the ones he'd already bribed. Having regained the public's love, his heart was beating once more. Who now would dare to compare themselves to him? He was the best. Basking in exhilaration at being at the top, he laughed aloud.

One day, a sudden piece of news shook him to the core. His father had been in a hit and run accident. The perpetrator wasn't identified. It was a case of messy interests and power struggles. But one thing was clear – his friends, the people who had nothing in their eyes but money, were responsible. But no, it was his fault. His bad decisions had piled upon one another, and finally, everything had exploded. Because of him, his father, who had done no wrong, was left in a vegetative state.

Once again, his world crumbled. He stopped all his activities and spent each day like a zombie. What did they say about true friends being by your side at your worst? Those people who had approached him because of his wealth, robbed him of whatever they could before abandoning him. The young man felt as though he'd been pushed off a cliff.

He had no one left. He'd lost the love of his life when he started taking drugs, and now, his father was unconscious in the hospital. It was the second car accident in his life. The pain of losing his eyes and his mother overwhelmed him once more.

Waves of regret crashed upon him. However, nothing could be undone. When he tried quitting drugs, his hands shook so badly he could never touch a piano again. What was left in his hand was not the smoothness of the piano keys, but something his friends had shoved towards him in a cruel act of ridicule – a jagged blade. He slowly lifted it to his wrist. And pulled hard.

'AHHHHH. STOP IT!'

As the bar sharpened into focus, Dae-il found himself on the floor, shaking uncontrollably.

'Haa— Haa—'

Gasping, he ran a hand down his chest several times to

calm himself down and checked his wrist. The spurt of blood gushing out was nowhere to be seen.

'W-what was that?'

His back was drenched in sweat. There were deep creases in his suit, and stray strands of hair escaped his ponytail. But this wasn't the time to think about appearances. Pulling himself out of this near-death experience was consuming all his energy.

'I told you. A bitter end,' said a deep voice.

Dae-il looked up at the unsmiling bartender and felt goosebumps running down his arm.

What am I doing here?

Dae-il was desperate to leave. He had to escape. Alarm bells were ringing in his head.

'I-I'll make a move. It's been great. Er, and—' His lips were still trembling as he pushed himself up from the floor. 'H-how much do I owe you? Is this enough?'

He dug out his wallet from his pocket, fumbling in his haste, so that it landed with a thud. The bartender picked it up and held it out to Dae-il.

'You've already paid.'

'I have?'

The bartender nodded. All right, it wasn't time to argue over this. As Dae-il was about to leave, the bartender spoke.

'It's now time to make a choice.'

'A choice? What are you talking about?'

'A choice of who shall die.'

Dae-il felt a tingle of electricity course through him. What was the man talking about? He must be a madman.

'Please walk towards the *mun* of your choice.'

The bartender tapped on his nametag before pointing at the back door.

'If you wish to die in his stead, come to me. If you'd like to leave the young man to die, open the door behind.'

It was like a cruel game of wordplay. To choose between Mun the bartender – a word that also means door – or the physical door behind. Who knows? There might a sword-wielding person lying in ambush behind the door. He'd better be careful.

He was also highly conscious of the rabbit pounding something in a mortar behind the bartender. A moment ago he had been sure that it was a young woman wearing bunny ears, but right now, it looked like a human-sized rabbit. When his eyes met the red irises of the rabbit, he couldn't help but let out a whimper of fear.

'Young man? What do you mean? Surely it can't be the person in my visions?'

'The very same one.'

A clipped answer without further explanations. This was ridiculous. It was merely a vision from a drunken episode. Who would ever sacrifice their life for a person they've just seen for the first time, not to mention in a vision? Dae-il was all the more certain that the bartender was not in his right mind.

'I-I also have loved ones. I have a child!'

A relapse of his habit to splutter whatever was on his mind. This time, he didn't care what he was saying as he inched backwards.

'All right, goodbye,' Mun said.

Dae-il thought he'd better hurry before the bartender changed his mind. He ran towards the back door and grabbed the knob. Luckily, it worked.

'Haa— phew.'

The door closed behind him. Wait, something was strange. He'd stepped outside, but he was still indoors.

'Huh . . .'

White tiles surrounded him. A long, straight corridor stretching into the distance reminded him of a gallery. Adding to that impression were the rows of paintings hanging on the walls on both sides.

Ding – Ding – Ding.

'Argh!'

The bells seemed to be hammering his ears. Like a startled meerkat, he shook his head vigorously. However, nothing out of the ordinary happened.

'Eh?'

The only strange thing was the door had disappeared. In its place was a pristine white wall. There was no trace that a door had ever existed.

'Was it all a dream?'

There was only one way ahead. Dae-il took cautious steps forward.

'The colours look familiar.'

He took a closer look. These were Park Dae-il's— his paintings.

'These aren't recent though.'

There was no trace of boldness or provocation. They were from the days when he still believed in his dreams. The paintings he'd truly enjoyed working on. Looking at them, one after the other, lifted his spirits. The debilitating anxiety vanished. There was such power in those paintings that the longer he walked, the happier he became.

'That's right. These are truly stories!'

He was enjoying himself. Now and then, memories bubbled

up as he walked down the corridor looking at the paintings. When he saw he was nearing the end of the corridor, a wave of disappointment washed over him.

And finally, the last painting.

That moment, he realised.

'Ah . . .'

At the end of a row of his most beloved paintings hung the very one which had left the deepest impression on him.

'Ahhhhh . . .'

It was the painting that had made him cry the moment he'd set his eyes on it. Only then did he remember. It hadn't been a painting. It was a photo.

'NO!'

He spun on his heels and ran with all his might. In the photo was a sleeping baby he held in his arms. His son. And in those features, he saw the boy in his visions.

'No, no way. Please. I was wrong.'

His breath was ragged. Several times he slipped, but he quickly picked himself up and continued running. Panting, he got back to where the door had been, but no matter what he tried, there was no sign of a handle. It was a stretch of white. There was no way of returning to the shop.

'I'm sorry. I said I'm sorry. Forgive me.'

Dae-il begged and begged. He got down on his knees, fervently rubbing his palms together in a plea as he broke down in tears by the wall.

'I'll gladly die. Take my life. I'll go to hell, just save my son. Please. I beg you.'

He howled in anguish. Tears streamed down as he pounded on his chest with his fist, wailing.

'Please, I beg you.'

His cries reverberated in the corridor, and suddenly, a voice spoke.

'Do you you really wish that?' It was the bartender.

While the bartender was nowhere to be seen, Dae-il could imagine the pitying look on his face.

'Yes, yes. I beg you. Please.'

Click. The wall, which had been a smooth white, opened. Dae-il hurriedly stepped through, and immediately, he knew he was back in the bar masquerading as a bookshop.

'Thank you. Thank you.'

Dae-il bowed his head at the bartender as he thanked him over and over. Mun held Dae-il's hands as he sobbed.

Mun spoke. 'You only have a single chance. Enter the book and change the story.'

On the table, what lay in place of the cocktail glass was a book. It had the same title as his drink: *The Boy Who Sees*. Dae-il was thrilled, as though he was looking at his son.

'What should I do to change the story?'

'The only person who can do that is the person who owns it.'

The bartender looked sombre. However, Dae-il wasn't about to give up. He would do anything for his child.

'Listen here,' said the bartender. 'No matter how close you are to a person, it's impossible to change someone else's story. In the end, it's up to them. The only person who can make the change is the young man.'

'Are you telling me to persuade him? To convince him—'

The bartender shook his head slightly. Dae-il waited for him to continue. The bartender's eyes bore into his.

'That's why I'm telling you to try your best.'

The bartender pushed the book into his hands.

'Park Kyungmin. Do you understand me?'

Swoosh—

The ground disappeared. He was free-falling. All he could do was to grab on tightly to the book as he screamed.

By the time his screams subsided, his throat was burning. He felt a zing in his fingertips. Shocked by the strange sensation, he released his grip, and with a clink, he heard something metallic rolling.

'W-what is happening?'

He looked left and right, but all was dark. That moment, he realised. He couldn't see. A chill ran down his spine. Before he could make sense of what was happening, a ringtone pierced the silence.

Du-ru-ru-du-dun~♬

A cheery tune. He recognised his own composition.

'Answer the call,' he said.

Immediately, the phone's voice assistant was activated, and the call connected.

'Park Kyungmin, you jerk! How much longer are you going to drown yourself in drugs?'

'Lee Eunjung?'

The three syllables he hadn't spoken aloud in a long time. The woman who'd left him. Just as he was about to dial up the speaker's volume, he was seized by a sense of unease. Over the phone, he could hear her sobbing.

'Your father. He passed away.'

'What?'

What was it that he'd experienced that day? Some time had passed, but the events were still vividly imprinted on his mind. The bar masquerading as a bookshop. The strange bartender. The server with bunny ears. He saw with his father's eyes, looked at things from his perspective. It almost felt like he *was* him. Was this all a dream? Or was it Father's last life lesson for him? To wake him up from his drugged stupor?

After he'd lost his sight, there were times other kids would whisper to one another in his presence. One day, he took out his anger on his father who had come to pick him up from school, snapping that he was embarrassed of him. He hadn't realised that from that day, his father started to painstakingly take care of his appearance.

Because his father was never good with words, Kyungmin had few memories of their conversations. All along, he'd thought that his father didn't care about him. The one time his father really spoke to – shouted at – him was when he had discovered that his son had turned to drugs. Feeling attacked by his father's aggressive words, Kyungmin screamed back, 'But you gave up on your dream too!'

At the time, he thought he had to protect his dream, and he'd do *anything*, no matter the consequences. To be number one, he thought that he had to stand out from the others; he had to be special. He arrogantly thought of himself as a one-of-a-kind, someone special and destined to be different.

He dismissed his father as a coward who didn't work hard enough for his dream. It was too late, but he finally realised how wrong he was. His father had sacrificed his dream to bring up a child by himself. The father he knew always stuck to his ideals. That he had given up on his dream and painted what he clearly abhorred made his chest tighten.

'Sit here. The keyboard is in front.'

Guided by his lover, he lowered himself onto the seat.

'Eunjung-ah.'

'Yeah?'

Just as she was about to walk away, he called out to her. He was always thankful for her presence. She was too good for him. Even if he were to borrow all the words in the world, he still wouldn't have enough to thank her.

'I'm always . . .'

'Thankful and sorry? Well, you should be.'

She chuckled softly and he felt a tingle of electricity trailing down his back when she smacked him lightly.

'Do well. Don't be nervous. I'm here rooting for you.'

A zing coursed through his heart. He remembered his mother saying the same before his football competitions. He carved her words onto his heart and nodded.

'Thanks.'

'Stop thanking me. Okay, I'm heading down.'

He felt her presence fade into the distance. Today was the debut performance of his new composition. He was nervous. Not because of the audience. In the silence during the performance, it didn't quite matter how many of them there were.

'Huu—' Kyungmin exhaled. He was nervous about the performance. He slowly raised his hands to the keys and felt the vibrations humming on his fingertips. Today, he wanted to tell a story with his music. The story of his father who, despite giving up on his dream in the harsh reality of life, was someone to be proud of – more so than anybody else. His father was successful, and Kyungmin was proud of him.

Ding—

The first note rang out with strength. The melody began

to dance, weaving together his father's life story. Kyungmin was thankful to the bartender with the striking blue hair. If not for him, he would never have seen his father's paintings.

Riding the dance of Kyungmin's fingers, his father's life and his story reverberated far and wide.

Chapter 2
Sausage Stir-Fry

'Bo-reum, bring me the vial of tears from the Tears Bunny, will you?'

The Moon Rabbit, who was sweeping the floor, jutted out her lip in annoyance as she mumbled, 'Isn't it just right in front of you . . .'

But once she entered his line of sight, her features automatically rearranged themselves into a bright smile. Picking up a small bottle from the tray, she held it out to him.

'What's this for?'

'The tears help to neutralise suffering. It'll make a sad ending less painful to swallow.'

Mun unscrewed the cap and peered into the bottle. The tear-shaped marbles shone a mesmerising blue.

'This should do.'

Nodding in satisfaction, he emptied the contents into a big mortar.

'I'll leave this to you.'

Mun patted her shoulder and held out a huge pestle that was thicker than two baseball bats put together. Looking at its girth, Bo-reum could already imagine how heavy it was. She let out a sigh.

'And you're just going to watch?'

'Of course. Then I'll know if you're doing a good job.'

Mun opened a folding chair and settled down comfortably with a book on his lap. It looked like he planned to enjoy a leisurely read while keeping a sharp eye on her.

'Huu—'

She allowed herself a moment to imagine swinging the pestle at his head.

He gets on my nerves, but oh well, I suppose he's still a good person, Bo-reum tried to convince herself as she adjusted her grip.

Exhaling a faint grunt, her bunny ears sprang to attention and rock-like muscles undulated beautifully on her arms. Her eyes gleamed blood red. A single look was enough to send anyone running in the opposite direction.

Kung, kung—!

The ground shook as she started pounding the mixture. Meanwhile, Mun leisurely turned the page.

'Shouldn't you be at the counter? What if a customer walks in?'

'Well, I don't see anyone.'

Bo-reum sighed. It'd been only a month since she started working at the shop, but this was enough time to realise that it was doomed to go under. So far, she'd seen a grand total of two customers. *Two.* And considering that the second person was the first customer's son, technically they only received a single payment.

It's a no-brainer.

Just like the saying that everything could be traced to an origin, it wasn't hard to figure out why their business was abysmally poor.

'Obviously because the boss sits around and does nothing.'

'Hmm? You said something?'

Bo-reum gave a start. 'Oh. Nothing!'

Grinning sheepishly, she averted her gaze. His ears were too sharp for his own good (and hers). It wasn't the first time he caught her muttering under her breath.

'Don't you think we should do some advertising? Hold a special event or something?'

'Yup, that's what we're preparing for.'

Her bunny ears perked up in attention. This was the best thing he'd said in the entire month. She looked at him eagerly and her gaze followed his finger pointing at the . . . mortar.

'Tears of the Tears Bunny. It'll make the cocktails easier to stomach. That's the special event. In any case, it's been bugging me to see Dae-il-ssi in so much pain.'

'If it bugged you that much, you should've added the tears to Park Kyungmin-ssi's drink!'

'What I served him wasn't alcohol but an antidote.'

If one became too drunk, it was possible to get completely absorbed in the story, Mun explained. That was what happened to Kyungmin – he thought that he was his father.

Thanks to the antidote, he became sober enough midway for the memories to return. As for the pain he'd felt, Mun added, it was his own anguish welling from his heart.

'Does that mean you took Park Dae-il-ssi's life as payment for the drinks?'

'How can we use a person's life as payment in kind?'

'Was that not what happened?'

'Dae-il-ssi was destined to die. He happened to chance upon our shop in his comatose state.'

'Then what did you get paid with?'

'You've seen them – the photo and his paintings.'

That was the payment? Till now, the Moon Rabbit had no idea how the shop operated. Naturally, she had more questions.

'When Kyungmin-ssi confused himself as his father, why did you make him choose between saving himself and his son's life?'

'Just raising the stakes. I told you, didn't I? The only person who can change a story is its owner. No one can choose on behalf of someone else. Of course, I also hoped that things would go according to Dae-il-ssi's wishes, but in the end, Kyungmin-ssi had to decide for himself.'

'What if Park Kyungmin, thinking that he was his father, chose to save himself and not his son? Would he then die, and Park Dae-il-ssi lives on?'

'Didn't I already tell you that Dae-il-sii was dying regardless? What Kyungmin decides can only affect his own life. I can only play a hand in dialling up the tension.'

Bo-reum was still confused. But even as the mess of thoughts continued to turn cartwheels in her mind, her hands didn't stop.

Mun glanced at her. 'How can you wield that huge thing with such ease?'

But Bo-reum wasn't paying attention. She was the type who'd filter out all distracting noise when she was mulling over something important. Suddenly, a question popped into her mind, and she turned around.

'Ahh!'

Instead, what escaped her lips was a yelp of shock. *Kung.* Bo-reum dropped the pestle. Mun glanced up from his book only to see the colour drain from the Moon Rabbit's face. Her sinewy arms shrank, and the red receded from her eyes.

Bo-reum was panickedly pointing towards a young girl who was standing in the doorway, looking just as wide-eyed.

'Wow . . .'

Unlike the Moon Rabbit though, the girl's eyes sparkled with excitement. Mun got up and slowly approached the girl. He was no longer wearing his bartender uniform. Instead, he'd transformed into a pastry chef

'I've found it, right? The magic shop.'

While the Moon Rabbit stood there gaping, Mun kneeled to the child's eye level and flashed a friendly grin.

'Can you tell me what's written here?'

Mun tapped a finger on his name tag. The little girl wrung her hands anxiously and cast him a furtive glance.

'Not sure? Then let me give you some options to choose from. One, Moon.'

She shook her head. Just as he was about to give her the second choice, the little girl pointed a finger at the door.

'It's *Mun* – the door that opens and closes,' said the child, holding her gaze steady.

Only then did Bo-reum exhale the breath that she was holding in.

Mun nodded. 'Indeed, my esteemed customer.'

No longer sounding like he was simply humouring a child, Mun's voice was now deeper, more formal. 'I'm sorry, but this is the staff area. Allow us to guide you to your table, please.'

Even before Mun could signal for her to come over, Bo-reum quickly stepped in to hold the girl's hand and bring her back to the dining area.

Bo-reum plastered on a bright smile, but it didn't hide the fact that she was still shaken. And when she saw the empty liquor glass on the table, her jaw dropped.

'Oh God. Don't tell me she . . .'

She was sure that just moments ago, the glass had held a cocktail with the most mesmerising colours. Even an adult would find it hard to resist, never mind a child.

It wasn't the girl's fault. If there was anyone to blame, it would be the irresponsible bartender who'd left it out in the open. Bo-reum glared at Mun, who simply shrugged.

'I was going to do a taste test, but I forgot about it.'

'Of all things?!' Bo-reum whispered from between clenched teeth.

Not wanting to scare the child, she continued to crinkle her eyes without realising that her strange facial expression could only make things worse.

Mun was his usual laid-back self as he returned to his position behind the counter separating himself from the girl who stood on the other side.

'Welcome, the Moon Glow Bookshop is where chance becomes destiny. That I accidentally left the drink out, and you emptied the glass, is all a part of what is meant to happen. Are you feeling all right?'

'Who is he kidding – *chance?* More like negligence. And it's not just any drink. How can he let a child touch alcohol?'

Mun ignored her mutterings.

'Is this really a magical shop?'

In the child's eyes was a mix of nervousness and anticipation. Mun clapped once and the rows of alcohol bottles vanished, replaced by a kaleidoscope of sweet drinks and ice-cream tubs. The girl stood awestruck at the rainbow-coloured display. Meanwhile, Bo-reum dropped her face into her palms.

'Welcome to the magical shop.'

Cheeks flushed in excitement, the young girl climbed up onto a stool and settled down comfortably.

'I've always wanted to visit a place like this. Ajusshi, are you a wizard? Can you grant me a wish?'

'Of course. Your wish is my command.'

Feeling an intense gaze boring into the back of his head, Mun turned to see fire spitting out of Bo-reum's eyes.

'Don't go around making empty promises to a kid,' she mouthed urgently. Mun smiled and deliberately ignored her. Even with his back towards her, he could feel her blazing stare.

'I want to be special! A very, very special person. Then I can make fire with a snap of my fingers, and I can guess what goes into a dish just by smelling it!'

'That sounds lovely.'

'Stop saying things that you can't be responsible for!' Bo-reum hissed.

This time, Mun looked at her. His lips moved, and he winked. It might seem like he was trying to reassure her, but that couldn't be further from the truth.

'Maybe it's time for a taste of bitter reality.'

Oh God. How could he say something like that in front of a kid? Her eyes flashed red, and her arm twitched.

'Can you really make my wish come true?' the girl asked.

'Of course. But would you also do me a favour in return?' Mun said as he brought the menu over. He tapped it twice and the alcoholic drinks in the menu vanished, replaced by an assortment of milkshakes and other sugary drinks.

'What do you need me to do?'

'You can start by placing an order.'

'Oh . . .'

'It'll be delicious.'

The child glanced up as if to double-check that it was okay to choose something, and reassured by his bright smile, she pointed at one of the drinks.

'Great choice. This one's guaranteed to be bursting with flavours. One moment, please.'

Picking up a zesty lemon, he squeezed out the juice and added some sugar. With a few snaps of his fingers, in no time, a bubbly drink was ready. On top, he sprinkled freshly ground blue powder which contained the magical tears of the Tears Bunny.

'Here's your order of the *Cosmos Fairy*.'

The colours shimmered. When Mun placed a piece of black drawing paper behind the glass, it was like looking up at the sparkling stars in the night sky.

'Wow.'

A soft murmur of awe escaped the child's lips. She reached for the straw and sucked greedily.

Fairies are beautiful, lovely, and always excel in whatever they do. But not me.

In between the sweetness was a sharp tanginess. Surprised, the child released the straw. She looked up at Mun, but he simply smiled. An odd thrill mixed with nervousness bubbled in her. A magical drink! Right in front of her!

'This is so fun.'

Images flitted across her mind when the sourness tickled her nose. It was as if sipping the drink already made her feel special, and her eyes lit up.

The girl held the straw between her lips once more and

sucked. *Gulp, gulp.* The burst of sourness had a hint of bitterness, but she was too excited to think of stopping.

The stars dazzled in the night sky. Big or small, they were all the work of fairies who busied themselves decorating the sky.

Just like how darkness couldn't blanket the light, the fairies' laughter filled a vacuum in the universe. Fairies are always a special presence, well-loved wherever they go.

Among the fairies was an extra special one. Or rather, because she was so different from the rest, 'unusual' might be the appropriate word.

She was much, much taller than the rest, and there was a sharpness in her gaze. The same could be said of her personality; she was quick-tempered. When she saw the others frolicking and showing off, she'd get annoyed. Because she found it hard to fit in with her peers, her parents were always worried about her. Even the strict teacher at school couldn't do anything.

'What do you even hope to become when you grow up?' To the question laced with exasperation, she'd confidently reply, 'I want to be a guardian of the universe.'

Guardians of the universe. They were at the frontline of protecting the stars, the planets and the galaxies. In her eyes, they were the strongest, the coolest. She only wanted to be a guardian, nothing else. However, her dream was quickly turned into the butt of a joke.

'Ha. Fairies can never be universe guardians. That's only for strong rabbits.'

It was a fact determined at birth. Everyone told her the same, saying that they only had her best interests at heart.

'It's for your own good. Stop dreaming the impossible. Just be like the rest of the fairies and learn how decorate the stars.'

The aching emptiness in her heart stretched infinitely like the universe, and it was as if an insurmountable gap stood between her and her dream. No matter how far she stretched her arm, it remained painfully out of reach.

'Didn't they always tell us that fairies can do anything?'

Misery filled her.

'Adults are liars.'

Her heart was a dark, empty universe.

Gulp. The girl swallowed the last drops. She touched the glass, as if sad to finish her drink.

'Can I get another one of these?'

'I'm sorry. We can only serve one drink to underaged customers.'

The girl fought back the urge to whine. If she threw a tantrum, she had a feeling that the wizard would not grant her the wish. She couldn't help but think of the fairy's story. The vivid images tugged uncomfortably at her heartstrings.

She was proud of herself for having read many fairy-tale books at school, but never had she come across a story with such a sad ending. She refused to accept that it ended like this; she needed to find out more.

'What happened to that fairy?'

'What do you think?'

While the girl was flustered at having the question thrown back to her, she thought about it carefully. If this was like the usual fairy tales she had read, it wasn't hard to guess the answer.

'A guardian is like the police of the universe, right? I think her dream will come true. Even though they say an ordinary fairy cannot be one . . . but she's special!'

'Sadly, she didn't become a guardian. She tried a couple of times, but it always ended in failure.'

'What? But if we try our best . . .'

'Aha. But there are some things in life that remain impossible no matter how hard you work.'

The child's face crumpled. Bo-reum, who'd been watching from the kitchen, looked horrified.

'What are you saying to a child?!'

Mun shrugged, as if saying: *If it's not going to work out, it's not going to work out.*

'Well, she didn't give up right from the start. Once, twice, three times, then ten, twenty, a hundred times – she kept trying, but her dream didn't come true. Finally, she ended up decorating stars like any other fairy.'

The significance of the efforts needed to even reach a hundredth attempt was lost on the young child. Instead, with a a touching innocence, she said, 'Maybe she'll make it at the hundred and first time.'

'The fairy was tired. She'd reached her limit and lost her will to keep trying. By then, much time had passed; the days of chasing dreams were over. Time bared its cruel fangs.'

Even though the girl couldn't completely understand what the fairy was going through, she nodded. Her parents would also say *no* to her, and she learned that when they did, no matter how hard she begged, nothing would change. And she gradually learned to accept that as a fact of life.

'Do you also have a dream?'

The girl nodded. Even before Mun asked, she answered, 'I want to be a chef!'

To children, whether their dream was realistic or not didn't matter. The little girl was proud to share her dreams.

'Then what if you're like the fairy in the story and your dream didn't come true?'

There was a loud clank in the kitchen. However, Mun didn't stop his cruel questions. With a glance at his watch, he continued.

'There can be many reasons. Maybe you just fell out of love with cooking. Or seeing others more talented made you feel small. Or you end up giving in to the social expectations and pressure of finding a so-called proper job.'

The young girl struggled to fully understand what Mun had said, but she thought to herself: What if, like the fairy, she couldn't be a chef for some reason? The idea made her gloomy. She pursed her lips tight as she fell into thought.

'But at the very least, I'll be able to make a sausage stir-fry, right?'

Bo-reum, who was aiming the pestle at Mun's leg, paused in surprise. Meanwhile, Mun nodded at her question.

The child shrugged. 'Then that's good enough for me. It's okay if I can't be a chef. But it'll be nice if I can at least make sausage stir-fry and kimchi stew. Sausages are my favourite, but Mummy only makes it sometimes. I feel a lot better when I eat it!'

The girl wanted to be a chef because yummy food always made her happy. Once, she rolled kimbap with her mum, and it was so delicious that she'd never be able to forget the taste. But what she was too young to realise was that it stood out in her memory because of an extra ingredient inside – her mum's lavish praise.

'Are you really going to be okay even if you can't be a chef?'

'I'll be sad. But there's nothing I can do, right? Mummy

says sadness and happiness are friends. Just like sausages and spinach. She tells me I can't pick just sausages, because they go hand-in-hand with spinach. It's okay, because if I eat the spinach, it means I'll get to have my favourite sausages!'

Mun wasn't sure how much the child understood him, but he liked her answer. Perhaps it'd be fine to ask her for the favour, he thought.

'Do you mind leaving a message for the fairy? She's very sad and I think she'll appreciate a word of encouragement.'

The child nodded gravely. She glanced up at Mun, who said he'd pass on the message.

'Er . . . Hi? Ms Fairy. I heard you're having a hard time. I know how that feels. I was very sad when I always failed to get full marks for spelling no matter how hard I practised. I think you're amazing. Even if you didn't become a guardian, you're doing a good job decorating the stars, right? It may not be what you want to do, but it's very cool that you're trying your best. My mum tells me that to be an adult means learning to do things well even though we may not enjoy it very much, so I think you're an amazing adult. But on days you feel extra sad, try eating sausages. It'll make you happier. It works for me!'

The girl paused and shyly gave a little dip of her head to indicate that she had finished. Mun returned her greeting with a bow.

'I feel the same way, too.'

His watch beeped. It was exactly noon.

Beep, beep—

The reverberations spread, getting louder and louder. The child's brows creased. The alarm ringing in her ears felt strangely familiar.

★

Beep, beep—
 'Ah.'

She must've dozed off. At the train announcement that the doors were closing, she quickly looked out the window. *Shit.* It was her station. She alighted just in time to hear the train doors close with a thud behind her.
 'Ugh.'

She stretched her stiff shoulders. The tight white blouse and heels felt suffocating. Because she'd worked late today, the subway station wasn't as crowded compared to the morning rush hour. Stepping through the turnstiles, her legs automatically headed in the direction of home.

She let out a sigh. 'I'm so stressed.'

Every day was a repeat of yesterday. The light in her was extinguished a long time ago. When she heard yet another ex-classmate had succeeded in achieving their dream career, instead of congratulating them heartily, her mood soured.

Since when have I changed so much?

Her self-esteem hit rock bottom. Again.

The streetlights illuminating the path and the bright glow slanting out from the shop windows made her feel even more alone in the darkness.

Letting out a soft sigh, she turned, and her gaze landed on something. Among the books on display in a shop window, her attention was drawn to one of them – *Introduction to Cooking.*

Have I been ordering takeout too often?

After a moment's pause, she stepped into the bookshop. Her footsteps seemed lighter than usual, and she had the curious sensation that someone was gently patting her on the back.

A fuzzy feeling spread in her heart, as though someone was

telling her: *You're doing great.* The gentleness gave her the curious, slightly awkward feeling that she was getting comforted by a child. And at the back of her mind, some of her childhood memories were slowly surfacing.

'Yeah, I'm doing a good job.'

She tried saying it aloud. The words of affirmation filled her chest with warmth. *That's right.* She was doing a good job. Even if she'd strayed so far away from her childhood dreams, even if she was clocking in and out of the office for the sake of making a living.

Today, she felt proud of herself. Taking out her phone, she dialled the first number on her favourite contacts. After a short connecting tone, a bright voice rang out.

'My dear daughter! Is something wrong?'

'Nothing. I just miss you, Mum.'

'Have things been tough?'

'No. Just thinking about you. Should I come home this weekend?'

'Of course! Is there anything you want to eat?'

'Oh, yes.'

'Tell me and I'll cook it for you.'

'Sausages. I've got a sudden craving for your sausage stir-fry.'

'Sausages?'

'And kimchi-jjigae.'

'*Aigoo.* How is my grown-up daughter still a child? All right, Mummy will have it ready when you come home.'

'Mum?'

'Yes?'

'I love you.'

★

'She wasn't a kid?'

Bo-reum felt scammed. With a frown, she glanced at the back door where the customer had walked out only a few moments ago. Mun cleared the empty glass and placed it in the washing-up bowl.

'She's probably a lightweight drinker and got too drunk. One glass was enough to knock her back to her childhood days. On the positive side, at least I didn't feed an under-aged kid alcohol, don't you agree?'

Mun flashed her a grin. From his attitude, it was clear that he'd known right from the start. Bo-reum felt like she was being made a fool of.

'And how did you know? That was deliberate, wasn't it? That *Cosmos Fairy* drink – are you talking about Pamina?'

The fairy who yearned to be a guardian of the universe, a job that was reserved for strong rabbits like Bo-reum.

'Looks like you know her?'

Bo-reum refused to meet his eye. 'She's so famous. It'd be weird if I didn't know her.'

Before he could say anything else, she quickly changed topic.

'How did you know she wasn't a kid?'

'Oh. The book I was reading was hers. When you were busy pounding the mixture.'

'What a coincidence.'

'Didn't I tell you already? Here is where chance turns into destiny. The timing was impeccable.'

Bo-reum had no idea how much of what he was saying was the truth. But from the way he didn't even bat an eyelid just now, he probably wasn't that trustworthy. Suddenly, an idea flitted into her head.

'Does that mean that the more you read, the more customers we'll get?'

This might be the opportunity to turn their dismal business around. Heck, she'd even be happy to read to him all day, every day. Of course, there was a reason why she was invested in making sure the business did well.

'If it were that straightforward, we'd have a full house by now.'

That was true. Come to think of it, she'd seen him reading in the past, but the shop had remained quiet.

Mun had the habit of finishing the last page of a book only to start from the beginning again. At first, she wondered if it was because he liked that particular book, but after seeing him do that for every single book, she found it rather odd.

However, she never asked him why. She wasn't that interested to know.

'Haa—' She let out a sigh.

So, his reading habit had nothing to do with getting customers. She deflated visibly. But there was something else she was curious about.

'What happened in the end? You read the book, didn't you? Did that customer end up becoming a chef? Or . . .'

Mun, who was sitting cross-legged on the chair, suddenly sidled up to her. She shrank back and looked at him.

'What are you doing?'

'Are you curious what happened next?'

Gulp. She swallowed hard. It was as if he was on the cusp of letting her in on a secret. With her gaze fixed on his lips that seemed to open and close mysteriously, she slowly nodded. He leaned forward and whispered into her ear.

'It's a secret.'

The tension vanished in an instant.

'I knew it.' She glared hard.

Mun chuckled, and the meaning was clear: *It won't be fun if I tell you now.*

She let out a long sigh.

A month had passed, yet Mun remained as enigmatic as ever.

Chapter 3
At the Crossroads

'Welcome.'

Bo-reum greeted the customer with a bright smile. However, she was on pins and needles. Of all the times, Mun had chosen this moment to step outside.

What impeccable timing!

She screamed inwardly, but on the outside, she maintained an inscrutable expression. Smoothly, she guided the customer to their seat. She cleared away the menu on the table. Instead, she opened a bottle of wine she found sitting in a corner of the kitchen.

'You can drink this if you're feeling a little down.'

Mun had told her that with a kind smile, before adding, 'But I'll deduct it from your salary.' She wished she could gulp down some right now, but she had to take care of the customer first.

And I can just get him to pay for it.

The Moon Rabbit filled the wine glass with a standard pour and set it down in front of the customer.

'Please enjoy your drink.'

She was doing a good job handling an unexpected situation, the Moon Rabbit reassured herself. But as the customer lifted the glass to his lips, she was struck by a sudden thought.

How am I supposed to get him to pay? She had been so preoccupied with making the sale that she hadn't thought of the next steps.

Up till now, Mun was the one in charge of handling the payments. She had no idea how much the drinks cost, or how customers were billed. So far, she'd only seen Mun make small talk with them, but when she asked him later, he'd said the payment was completed.

Same with Dae-il-ssi's visit. She only took her eyes off them for a moment, and when she next looked up from the mortar, the customer was gone, and Mun was left with the photo and the paintings. That young child, too. She'd seen Mun hold a red sausage-shaped jewel, calling it 'sincere words of encouragement'.

'What a lovely aroma.'

The man lifted his sharp chin and downed the wine in one shot. He had a clear, gentle voice that spoke of trustworthiness. Bo-reum felt a little more at ease.

Or rather, it was his gold wristwatch, and the expensive-looking frames perched on his nose that were trustworthy. While she had no idea how much the wine cost, the man looked like he could afford it. There was only one thing left to do.

Keep him here until Mun returns.

Bo-reum smiled. 'Would you like another glass?'

'Yes, please.'

He knocked it back, and like the first time, the emotions that he'd forgotten seemed to resurface in his mind. Not wanting that feeling to slip away, he continued asking for the wine, each time emptying the glass in one gulp. Soon, he finished the entire bottle.

'What an interesting wine. Brings me back to the old times.'

Back to the childhood days where he drew on brick walls with small pebbles. With each scratch of the white line, the children's giggles filled the alleyway. Who would imagine that a kid playing in the back alleys would grow up to be so successful? He didn't even have to look that far back. Even until his early twenties, no one would have imagined that he'd become a 'genius writer'.

He thought back to the days living in a tiny room, so cramped that he could barely stretch his limbs, and the old, musty smell that hung in the air. Because he wasn't working a so-called proper job, poverty was his closest friend. He owned nothing, but life blessed him with a single stroke of good luck – his wonderful girlfriend.

'Cliff, I love you.'

The words she whispered into his ears were sweeter than honey, more melodious than any music. He licked his lips. The aroma of the wine lingering between his teeth reminded him of her loveliness.

'What's the name of this wine?'

Only then did Bo-reum glance at the label. A frown flashed across her features, disappearing just as quickly, and she replied smoothly, 'First Love's Kiss.'

'How interesting.'

Not *first kiss* as one might have expected, but a first love's kiss. He chuckled. How cumbersome. If it were him, he'd have pared down the word count.

In his light-headed euphoria, he spent some time musing over the name. Suddenly, he thought of another interpretation. When he thought of his first kiss, he naturally thought of his first love. Those lovely times remained vivid in his memories.

But his first love's kiss? His first love might have kissed someone else. *First love.* The first taste of romance is sweet, lovely, but also immature. It wasn't unusual to hear of first loves ending in failure. He was no different. In the passing years, perhaps his first love had found someone new.

His jaw tightened involuntarily. He hated to admit it, but after all these years, he still couldn't get over the girl who'd smiled at him ever so sweetly.

'Helen.'

The name that had been swirling in his mind escaped his lips. He let out a bark of laughter. Seeing how he was drunk enough to utter her name aloud, it was probably time to head home.

'Can I get the bill?'

'Er . . . Um . . .'

The waitress glanced nervously at the back door. Cliff was confused. Did she want a tip?

He took out several notes and placed them beneath the glass. However, she still looked upset.

'Is there a problem?'

Her face flushed a beetroot red. That moment, there was a creak, and the back door swung open. Only then did she let out a sigh of relief.

Following her gaze, Cliff drew in a sharp breath. Standing at the door was a young man with striking blue hair.

As a writer, sometimes he experienced moments where he could immediately visualise someone's job, their personality, and flesh out an entire story in that instant. Even despite it being the first time meeting that person; even if he didn't know their name.

Of course, his imagination might not come close to the truth. But what was important to Cliff wasn't the truth – all he was after was a gripping story.

'Boreum-ah, can you help me with this?'

The waitress hurried out from behind the counter to take the stack of books in his hands. Swiping away the beads of sweat on his forehead, the enigmatic young man flashed Cliff a smile. His name tag read: *MUN*.

Cliff, who was about to get up, shifted awkwardly back into his seat and returned his smile.

'You dyed your hair?'

Aha. What an obvious question. Cliff ignored the self-deprecating voice inside him.

Rather than a sky blue, the man's hair was darker. Staring at it made Cliff feel as if he was being sucked into the depths of the ocean. His heart gave an involuntary lurch.

'I did. I wanted a lighter colour, to be like my younger brother. But my hair was originally green, so the blue came out darker than expected.'

Cliff had been nodding along, but at the last bit, he tilted his head in confusion.

Originally green?

He'd never met a person born with green hair.

Is he saying that he dyed it green, and then switched to blue? What about his brother? Did he dye his hair blue, or was he born with blue hair?

A ludicrous thought, but it fuelled his imagination. A story formed in his head.

Because of a gene mutation affecting melanin levels, a

young man was born with a striking hair colour, and he grew up with an obsession with colours. For him, his lover also dyes her hair the same colour. One evening, seeing everyone drenched in the colours of sunset, she smiles and says, 'Now we're all the same.' . . . The woman's smile continued to linger in Cliff's mind.

'Is there something else you need?' Mun asked.

'Ah. No, I'm good.'

Realising that he'd been staring, Cliff quickly shook himself out of his reverie. It'd been a long time since a story came to him in an instant. Eager to share it with someone, he quickly took out his phone, only to realise that there was no one to call. Helen had already left him.

Ever since he was a kid, Cliff had had a rich imagination. The adults smiled indulgently whenever he told one of his stories. Pleased as Punch, he spent even more time making up new ones. And because he didn't want to forget the stories, he started to write them down.

The habit continued into adulthood, but the reactions he got couldn't be more different.

'You're not a child any more. It's because you spend all your time daydreaming, that's why you can't find a job!'

He had hoped that things would be different after he became an author. Surely the people working in publishing would appreciate his stories. However, the feedback he got was dispiriting – 'the plot's too predictable', 'it's stale.'

Only when one of his books became a bestseller did people start to take notice of him and his stories, but by then, he'd mastered the art of closing himself to others. Outside of the few people he worked with, he grew reluctant to talk about his ideas or stories with others.

A wave of bitterness swelled up. These days, writing no longer brought him the same joy. He wrote with the sole purpose of attracting the readers' attention, and what he came up with made him feel so empty, as though the stories themselves were also full of holes.

This one's good though.

The images that came to him at the sight of the young man with striking blue hair wasn't another empty story, but one that he was inspired to write from the heart.

If only I could share this with someone!

The alcohol was making his heart beat faster, and he had a reckless impulse to dial a random number just to talk about it. His gaze landed on the stack of books that the young man had come in with.

'I take it that you enjoy reading?' Cliff asked.

The bartender nodded. 'I do.'

Cliff was elated but tried not to show it.

'What kind of books do you enjoy?'

'Novels are my favourite.'

In his excitement, Cliff knocked over the wine glass.

'Whoops!'

At that moment, he had the most peculiar sensation that time slowed down. The bartender's hand glided past Cliff's widened eyes and grabbed the glass before it toppled over. Thankfully, the glass didn't break, but the last few drops of wine danced in the air before landing on the table.

'A book I enjoyed recently is *The Unbreakable Red Thread*,' the bartender answered as he calmly took a dry dishcloth and wiped away the droplets.

Cliff's expression brightened, as if the last bit of reservation in his heart were also being wiped away. To think this young man had read his work! It was a romance novel he published around the time he was starting to gain popularity.

'I read that, too. Do you have a favourite scene?'

Cliff didn't let slip that he'd written the book. Instead of empty compliments, he wanted to know what this man really thought of it.

Is it the last scene where the protagonists reunite? Or when the main male character's secret is revealed?

Despite his thrumming heart, he tried to look calm and waited for the man's answer. After a moment's pause, the bartender spoke. 'He failed yet again. The first couple of times, he didn't let it get to him and worked even harder. However, with passing time, he felt worthless. The long string of failures knocked him down again and again, reducing him to a pitiful existence.'

Cliff was stunned, and doubly so. First, the bartender was quoting the exact lines in his book, and second, from a completely unexpected part.

It was the beginning of the novel where Cliff described the male protagonist's life alone. The story had barely started; the main female character had yet to appear! Among the many other scenes in the novel, why had this man chosen this particular one?

'If you don't mind me asking, did you only read the front part of the novel?'

'I finished it, cover to cover.'

'Ah. But why . . .'

'It might be a few lines in the novel, but in reality, I imagine that it mustn't have been easy getting through that period, right?'

Cliff had never thought about it from that angle. Because

he favoured a happy ending, he liked to have his protagonists enjoy huge success in the latter half of the book.

It was perhaps an unconscious reflection of Cliff's own life to write his characters suffering in the beginning, and to create a more dramatic turn of events later.

'As readers, we'll have faith that the protagonist's life is going to get better, but in the story, the character faces the very real anxiety of not knowing what's ahead of him. I tend to also enjoy the bits before the happily-ever-after in fairy tales. Reading about the characters' struggles and how they're trying their best to keep going helps me process a lot of my own feelings.'

Cliff nodded. Indeed, this young man had a unique aura about him. Thanks to him, he might try to write his next book from a brand-new perspective.

'What about you? Do you have a favourite scene?' Mun asked.

It was a little embarrassing to be talking about his favourite scene from his own novel, but he tried to sound as natural as possible.

'Ah. I like the part where he realises his mistake and reaches out to her again.'

The bartender returned the clean glass to him. Cliff rubbed the base absentmindedly and as it moved slightly, it gave off a clear tinkle.

'I also regret letting my ex go. I took her for granted and made a grave mistake. How I wish I could return to the past and fix what I did. Wouldn't that be great?'

Cliff was jealous of the male protagonist. His character wasn't a fool like him. So he lived vicariously through their story, witnessed how they surmount all obstacles to share a beautiful kiss at the end. However great the sense of satisfaction, it wasn't his own. As he'd put down his pen, the heavy loneliness hanging in his room filled his every breath and made his heart ache.

'Can I get another glass?'

'Of course. You can pick something from here,' said the bartender, holding out the menu.

For a small shop, they had quite a substantial menu.

If I had known, I'd have tried different drinks.

Despite the slight disappointment, he didn't make a fuss. The wine that the waitress had poured for him was delicious.

'How interesting.'

There were several categories, each related to an emotion. Of course, he had no idea that previously, they were categorised by their backdrops, like the universe and the Wild West period.

He looked at the drinks under THRILL – *Hidden Exam Paper, Free Fall, Hide-and-Seek*. From the names alone, it was impossible to imagine how they might taste. He was intrigued.

Under LONGING, he spotted the wine he'd had just now. *First Love's Kiss*. He smiled and as his gaze trailed down the menu, a soft *ah* escaped his lips.

'I'll have this, please,' he said, pointing at a drink under REGRET.

The bartender nodded lightly.

With an hourglass-shaped jigger, he poured streams of liquid into the silver shaker. Cliff watched his movements, mesmerised.

He closed a cup on top of the silver shaker and shook it. Cliff could hear the ice rolling as the shaker moved in a dance, and when it was tossed into the air, Cliff let out a sharp exhale of awe. And just when Cliff thought the shaker was going to drop, the bartender caught it with ease. Cliff breathed a sigh of relief. The cocktail was poured out and set in front of him.

'Your order of *A Different Choice* is ready.'

It was like the drink was tailored just for him. How he yearned to return to the days when they were in love. This time round, he wouldn't make the same mistake. He imagined holding tight to her hands and never letting go.

'What a delicious fragrance.'

The cocktail was stronger than he expected. His brows tightened as a stream of heat glided down his tongue, passing his throat and pooling in his stomach; it was almost as if he could trace its path.

'Whoa, a stiff one. I can feel my throat burning. May I have some water?'

'Here you go.'

Cliff gulped down the water. However, it didn't douse the fire in him. In fact, he could feel it intensifying.

Huu—

Each time he exhaled, the heat rose up to the back of his throat, making him even dizzier. He could tell that something was very wrong, but he could barely steady himself. All he could do was rest his head, which felt like exploding, on the table.

'Ugh—'

He must've had too much to drink. He shifted slightly, using his arm as a pillow for his heavy head, which provided a modicum of relief.

As the spinning gradually came to a stop, he tried to look up. However, he was seized with the sensation that the world was collapsing instead.

'Huh? Ahhhhhhhhhh!'

He was falling from a great height. There was no chair, no table, and not even the ground – everything seemed to have vanished in an instant. As the sounds of the wind whipped past his ears, his head cleared a little. He turned, but there was no sight of the alcohol bottles or the wooden shelves in the shop. All around him was the blue sky. He screamed, but it was as if someone was forcing his jaw shut.

'Ugh, uggh.'

With his mouth clamped shut, the screams reverberating in the air stopped abruptly.

I'm going to die.

Cliff screwed up his eyes tight. Suddenly, his feet touched something. His eyes flew open; he was standing upright on the ground.

'Are you even listening to me?!'

He jumped at the sudden voice. But the shock was nothing compared to when he saw who it was.

The golden locks, the high bridge of her nose. It was her – the woman for whom his heart ached in longing.

'Helen?'

'Whatever. I've had enough.'

From her red-rimmed eyes, tears streaked down her cheeks. Helen grabbed the coat on the sofa and walked out, slamming the door hard behind her.

'What's going on . . .'

Cliff raised a hand to his temple. The dizziness had completely receded, but he still couldn't make sense of what was happening. It was like a scene that came right out of a writer's imagination. Or rather, anyone who knew regret would've dreamt of something like this. Where he stood now was his old, tiny room, where he had shared many memories with Helen.

'How is it still the same? It's been five years already . . .'

From what he knew, the old building had been torn down for redevelopment. The room, as it was in his memories, didn't exist any more. However, everything was the way he remembered it, even the plain calendar on the wall. The musty smell in the cramped space was stirring his memories.

Zinggg—

Feeling a vibration in his pocket, he pulled out his phone only to see that it was an old model that he had used in the past. Someone was calling. A string of numbers appeared on the screen, an unsaved number. However, he knew exactly who it was.

'Hello? May I speak to Cliff, please? This is about the manuscript you submitted to our publishing house.'

It was his longtime editor. However, he was acting like this was the first time he was speaking to Cliff. He introduced himself, explaining the purpose of his call. That moment, it clicked.

'I've gone back to the past!'

'Sorry? What did you say?'

Without answering, Cliff tossed his phone aside and rushed out of the door.

Huff, huff—

It was a cold winter day. He'd run out without a coat. The biting wind felt like knives stabbing at him. However, he had no wish to turn back. Instead, he swung his limbs and ran even faster, until he was panting hard, his ears and cheeks flushed red. Even then, he didn't stop. Because he spotted her ahead.

'Helen!'

He shouted at the top of his voice. People on the streets stared, murmuring to one another, but Cliff didn't care.

'Helen!'

He called out with all his strength. She paused and slowly turned around. Her eyes widened.

'What are you doing? Are you planning to freeze to death?'

Tears swirling in her eyes, she hurried over, unwound her scarf, and tucked it around his neck.

Unlike the passers-by who flicked him odd glances, her first concern was to make sure that he wouldn't fall sick in the cold, even if they were just having an argument moments ago. Helen was that kind of person. Always warm and affectionate. He missed her so much. Tears threatened to spill from his eyes.

'I'm sorry, Helen. I know what day it is today. It's our seventh anniversary. I'm sorry that I was so obsessed with getting a publishing contract that it slipped my mind. And not just that – you tried your best to communicate with me, but I was constantly irritable. Like the fool I was, I didn't listen. I put my own pride first. In my eyes, all I could see was the contract, the money; I failed to see that I was making you cry. I'm sorry, I'm truly sorry.'

'Cliff, what—'

He pulled her into his arms. Even if it was a dream, it was okay. As long as he could seek her forgiveness, hug her once more, it was enough.

The bitterness that was embedded in his heart had grown over the years. He felt it in his bones – the foolishness of his arrogance, the gaping loss. He should've never taken her for granted.

'Helen, I'm sorry for what I did. You're my biggest blessing in life. Please don't ever leave me.'

As he said the words aloud, it was as if he was coughing out the hardened bitterness in his heart, like the heat that rose behind his throat after a stiff drink. He sobbed softly and the next moment, she hugged him back.

Helen chuckled. 'Cliff, sometimes you're really like a child.'

It was so easy. Why was it that he couldn't do it back then? In her warm embrace, he gradually relaxed and, hand in hand, they returned to his room.

'You're always my number one priority,' he said.

There was a saying that success was not just about talent, but also luck and timing. In this timeline, Cliff's novel failed to gain popularity. In fact, it was an embarrassing flop.

However, he had no regrets. To him, success wasn't about money. He gave up writing and found a stable job. It wasn't easy, but he was hardworking, and he earned enough to make ends meet. And they got married.

It would be a lie to say that they never had any more arguments. They still did, occasionally, but the difference was that they learned to resolve the issue together.

A Different Choice. Sometimes, Cliff would think about the bartender. He still couldn't believe that a miracle had happened to him.

'Congratulations. It's a boy.'

He had thought that nothing would shake him as much as the moment of realisation that he'd travelled back in time. But when he saw his son for the first time, he was grateful that life had given him another miracle.

The baby cried.

'Darling, you're amazing. It's been hard on you.'

He carefully cradled the baby in his arms; the little thing couldn't even open his eyes properly. *Thump, thump.* Feeling his son's tiny heartbeat, the tears spilled out of his eyes.

His child was beautiful in every way possible. His tiny wriggling fingers were the most adorable Cliff had ever seen, and the way his lips moved felt as though his precious child was going to speak at any moment.

'Tut, tut, tut.'

Was his son imitating the sound of a knock? How clever!

Cliff smiled down at his bundle of joy, and once again, the child moved his lips. This time, he spoke in a clear voice.

'Time to wake up, Cliff-ssi.'

A surge of anxiety blanketed him. *Tut, tut, tut.* The sounds seemed to reverberate in his head. Like an earthquake, the world was shaking. And the child moved his lips once more.

'Cliff-ssi, are you okay?'

'Ugh.'

Thud—!

If not for the bartender holding on to him, Cliff would've rolled onto the floor. With widened eyes, he looked wildly around him. Colourful bottles lined the wooden shelves. He looked down at his arms. No baby. Only his expensive gold wristwatch.

'W-what . . .'

'The drink must've knocked you out. My apologies. I should've warned you.'

With his help, Cliff returned to his seat. He accepted the glass of water from the waitress. So, he hadn't returned to the past. It was just a dream. He felt a stabbing disappointment.

'Looks like you had a good dream?'

'What?'

'When the dream is so good, it's cruel to wake up from it.'

Cliff laughed hollowly. Indeed, a cruelly good dream. His heart ached so much that he thought he might have been better off having a nightmare.

'What was the dream about?'

'I dreamt that I returned to the past. To five years ago, where I had the chance to repair my mistake.'

'Ah. Is this about your ex-girlfriend?'

'Yes. Maybe because it was a dream, we patched things up smoothly. I apologised and immediately, she forgave me. Would that be possible in real life?'

Cliff glanced up at the bartender with red-rimmed eyes. It wasn't clear if it was because of the dream, or his yearning for the past, but his expression spoke of desperation for some comfort.

'There are many things that can cause a fight between couples, but most of the time, it isn't a major issue but neglect. Hurt and disappointment cut deeper from a loved one. But if she sees how you're reflecting on yourself, I'm sure she'll forgive you.'

Cliff nodded slightly. His eyes were still bloodshot, but he no longer seemed trapped in the dream.

'We were together for seven years. Five years have passed since then, but I guess it's still not enough time to forget her.'

'Don't blame yourself, Cliff.'

Cliff felt the pressure in his chest ease a little. The bartender's striking blue hair and enigmatic aura now felt like a friend. It was their first meeting, but having opened up to him about his deepest feelings, Cliff felt a sense of closeness to this young man. How embarrassing it was that he'd approached him for the mere object of getting inspiration for his next work. To make it up to him, Cliff thought he wanted to share a little more about the dream. It felt as though it was okay to tell this man, even if it was just his delusion.

'In the dream, I chose her. And even when my writing career flopped, I never once regretted it.'

The bartender smiled. 'What's your definition of success?'

Cliff was stunned. *Success*. Wasn't it obvious? It was about money.

'Success . . .'

Cliff fell into deep thought. Since when did he begin to equate success with money? It looked like living a poor life had also made his heart empty. That he could no longer find inspiration these days was probably because instead of conveying a message through his writing, he was only seeking the wow factor.

'To me, success is crafting stories that touch the heart. The kind of writing that will bring a smile to my loved ones' faces.'

Cliff had thought that he loved words and writing more than anything else. But when he thought about it, what he loved was seeing the smiles of people who heard his stories.

That unbridled joy he'd experienced as a child surfaced from the deep recesses of his heart.

'Come to think of it, I have many regrets. There are many things I wish I could've done differently. If there was a time machine, I think it'd run out of battery in no time because of me.'

'Because we only live once, that's why life is beautiful, isn't it?'

Not a perfect life, but a beautiful one. The corners of his

mouth lifted. The young man with striking blue hair had indeed given him a lot of inspiration.

'If you ever decide to switch careers, I think your words would be as sweet and fragrant as your cocktails.'

Cliff stretched his arms. It was time to go home. Tomorrow, he had an important meeting. He peered at the bartender's name tag.

'If you don't mind, can I call you Mun?'

'Of course.'

'I'll drop by occasionally. It'd be lovely to have a chat again.'

Smiling, Cliff stood up. Mun returned the smile.

Cliff held out his credit card to Mun, and with the beep on the terminal, he paid the bill for his drinks. For some reason, the waitress next to Mun rounded her eyes in surprise.

'I hope you will make the choice that you won't regret, Cliff-ssi.'

Ding. With a tinkle, the door opened and closed. The chilly wind caressed his cheeks, but he didn't feel cold at all. With light steps, he was about to make his way home when a thought crossed his mind.

'Did I tell him my name?'

'Yes, I'll be there soon.'

'Great. Those people are extremely particular about being on time. See you in a bit, then.'

Cliff slipped his smartphone back into his pocket. The temperature had dropped considerably. If he didn't hurry, it felt as though his ears would be frozen the next minute.

As he passed a row of shops, he occasionally checked his appearance in the windows. He couldn't believe that his novel might very soon be adapted for the big screen. The director who approached him was a well-known figure with several hits to his name. But he was also rumoured to be extremely fastidious.

'Oh?'

He stood at the busy crossroads, waiting for the lights to change. And in that moment, among the crowd of pedestrians, his gaze met hers. Like destiny.

'Helen!'

She smiled. The intervening years had blunted the resentment between them. She touched the scarf wrapped around her neck and nodded at him in greeting.

'It's been a long time. How have you been?'

'Er . . . I . . .'

The initial moment of delight was gone. In its place was an awkward pause hanging between them. Cliff tried to say something, but his tongue was stiff.

'Er, how have you been?'

'Good. Oh, sometimes I hear about you.'

'Really?'

'Or rather, I read the interview you gave as a bestselling author.'

'Oh, I see.'

For a moment, it looked like he'd killed the conversation, but luckily, Helen was, as usual, adept at turning around the mood. Thanks to her, the conversation flowed, and they chatted about what they'd been up to, whether they were seeing anyone and where they were heading to.

She congratulated him heartily on the opportunity for a movie adaptation. Cliff couldn't suppress a smile upon hearing that she was single.

'Oh. It's a green light,' she said.

The pedestrians started moving forward.

However, they were not heading the same way.

'In that case . . .'

It was time to say goodbye. Cliff quickly asked for her phone number. Smiling, she gave it to him.

'I'll call you. Let's meet again,' he said.

She nodded. But he couldn't shake off the gnawing anxiety that if they parted here, he'd never see her again.

'Goodbye.'

She turned and headed her way. The opposite direction from Cliff. He glimpsed the faint smile on her face. Cliff knew that smile. It was the expression she made when she had to swallow what she wanted to say.

Cliff looked in the direction he was supposed to be heading. The gold watch weighed heavy on his wrist, as though reminding him that he was running late for his appointment. If he didn't hurry, his dream would crumble.

'Dream. That's right. *Dream.*'

The green man was flashing. Time was running out. He ran. The biting wind whipping his cheeks reminded him of that comforting dream.

'Helen!'

The lights changed and the cars started moving. The pedestrians went their ways. The only people left at the traffic lights were the two of them.

'Cliff?'

'Do you want to grab dinner? Not next time, but today. Right now.'

It was a short distance, but because he'd ran in a burst, he hunched forward, panting heavily. But he forced his lips to keep moving. He didn't want to make the same mistake. He didn't want to let go of his dream. The one right in front of him.

'I . . . I mean . . .'

As he tried to catch his breath, he looked up at her. The anxiety of perhaps getting rejected was making him tremble, but he didn't avert his gaze.

'Cliff, sometimes you're really like a child.'

A smile lit up her face. Not the faint smile where she looked like she was swallowing her words. The warmth that he yearned for, that would push back even the coldest of winds, was right in front of him.

Chapter 4

How to Make Cocktails

Ding, cha-ching. Ding, cha-ching.

Bo-reum was opening and closing the cash register at the counter, looking extremely disgruntled. It wasn't like she didn't know how to use it; she'd worked several part-time jobs in the past. To think she came up with all kinds of ridiculous antics to hold the customer back until Mun's return! As far as she knew, Mun had been taking payment in kind, so she'd never considered the possibility of a card or cash payment.

'Can't you put the prices in the menu? It'll make it so much easier to settle the bill.'

'But every customer pays a different price. What am I supposed to write in the menu?'

He's at it again.

Her face scrunched up like a crumpled piece of paper. Mun's answers could be frustratingly cryptic at times.

Same with the menu. There were two menus – one categorised by emotions, the other by the backdrop of the stories. Whenever a customer came in, Mun would hand her one of the menus, but she had no idea how he decided which one to use. That was why she hesitated to give the man a menu. Not that she knew how to make any of the drinks.

Thinking that she should at least learn how to hand out the right menu, she asked Mun, only to get back a non-answer.

'Grab whichever catches your eye. The story will find its way to the customer.'

'But what if I picked the wrong menu?'

She was looking all serious, but Mun, who was fiddling with the small bottles on the counter, ignored that and instead threw her another question.

'Have you been to a bookshop?'

'A bookshop?' she echoed. 'What's with a bookshop? Well, I've worked in one.'

'Is there any place you haven't worked in? Anyway, so I take it that you've bought a book before?'

'Yeah, of course, there are so many things I have to learn.'

Mun smiled, snapping his fingers as if it was the answer he was looking for.

'Exactly! And you aren't going to buy a book you've read before, but a new one, right? Have you ever opened a book with zero expectations but by the last page, it's gripped your heart? That was how I discovered my all-time favourite book. The small bookshop I was at didn't carry the title I wanted, so I ended up browsing and picking up something else. A real stroke of good luck.'

'So how is this related to my question about the menus?'

'If I had gone to a bigger bookshop, I would've bought what I wanted. But that means I would've missed the opportunity to discover the other book. It's this kind of serendipity that I want my customers to experience.'

Bo-reum scrunched up her face as she glanced down at the two menus on the table.

'But these days, only the big players survive, bookshops

too. Isn't it better to reduce the number of drinks and combine them into a single menu? When the shop is doing better, you can add the items back and make a larger menu.'

'You may have a lot of experience, but you're painfully unromantic. It's never about how strong the drinks are, but the vibes and the experience.'

Bo-reum massaged her throbbing temples. Once again, she was convinced that Mun was the reason business was so poor. She sighed heavily, but he continued to smile.

'Don't worry. Like I said, here is where chance becomes destiny.'

If it wasn't for that certain clause in her contract, she might've been happy to let things be. *On months when the sales exceed a certain amount, the employer is obliged to pay an extra allowance on top of the agreed salary.* Right now, when every single cent mattered to her, it was impossible not to fret over their dismal business.

'Ah, we ran out of this,' Mun murmured.

He shook the bottle, but didn't hear the familiar rattle. He glanced at the rest of the ingredients; the bottles were almost empty.

'We don't even have customers. Where did the ingredients go?'

Because she was still upset, the words that shot out of her mouth were sharper than she had intended. She cast a careful glance at her boss, but he didn't seem upset. In fact, he was beaming.

'I've been taking online orders. Looks like the response has been better than expected.'

'Online orders?'

This was the first time Bo-reum was hearing about it.

Her jaw dropped. Was it possible that she might get a little bonus this month?

'Manager Mun...'

She felt a rush of respect towards Mun. As she should – he was the owner, a true leader and visionary!

She wiped the tables with more vigour.

'Let's go shopping for ingredients,' Mun said.

Bo-reum bobbed her head. 'Sure! You have a strong rabbit here at your service.'

With a burst of focus, her eyes shone red as she flexed the rock-like muscles on her arms. He nodded in satisfaction. In that case, he should get everything at one go, and more.

Tears Bunny's Tears – 2 litres x 36 bottles
Dimples of Smiles – 62 pairs
Daytime Yawns – 186 times
Boiling Anger – 32 flasks

Humming a tune, Mun struck off each item with a red pen as they weaved from shop to shop. Mun turned around to see Bo-reum wheezing, buried under a sack of ingredients bigger than herself.

'Take a break here. I'll be back. There's someone I have to meet.'

Immediately, Bo-reum slumped onto a bench. Thick rivulets of sweat ran down her face as she gulped down the canned drink Mun had gotten for her from the vending machine. Finally, she felt a little more alive.

'Are there more things to buy?'

'Nope. Just going to make a quick stop somewhere before

going back. I might take a while; do you want to head back alone?'

Bo-reum shook her head. 'It's okay. I'll rest here and wait.'

She lay down on the bench.

As Mun's footsteps died away, Bo-reum closed her eyes. The breeze caressed the limp fringe plastered to her forehead.

'Ahh-haaa—' She yawned widely. The wind carried off the beads of sweat and her eyelids were drooping. With the weight lifted from her shoulders and her breaths less harried, she started to pick up more sounds from the surroundings. The faint noises from the street vendors, and closer to her, the birds chirping a lullaby. Leaves rustled in the wind. Basking in the gentle tickle of the sunshine, her eyelids fluttered to a close . . .

'Excuse me?'

'I'm not sleeping!'

Bo-reum jerked awake. She cast bleary glances around, but Mun was nowhere to be seen.

'Right here.' The voice was coming from below.

She looked down to see a pink rabbit.

'Excuse me, I believe you're the Moon Rabbit, the guardian of the moon. Are you Dae Bo-reum?'

The pink rabbit's eyes flicked up at Bo-reum's long white ears. At the mention of guardians, Bo-reum was a little embarrassed. She had left that job a long time ago. What had been the dream job of Pamina the fairy, felt to her like clothes that didn't quite fit her properly.

Swallowing the bitterness, she replied, 'I've quit. I'm working at a small shop now.'

Unexpectedly, the pink rabbit clapped in joy.

'Aha! Yes, I've heard that you're working on earth now.

I have questions for you,' she said, and added in a small voice, 'If it's not too rude of me to ask.'

Unlike Bo-reum, who looked human except for its bunny ears, the pink rabbit was a rabbit about the height of a small child, and instead of fur, it looked like it was made of pink droplets. One fell onto the ground, but it didn't make a wet mark. Immediately, Bo-reum knew that the rabbit was a Tears Bunny.

'My name is Bato. I'm a sales consultant for tears, and I'm in charge of the earth account. Oh well, not that I've ever been!'

For the next several minutes, the rabbit launched into a tirade about its job. Its friend, who worked at the warehouse for the tears, was simply whiling its time away – there were no sales – while getting the same pay. Meanwhile, Bato was stuck working round the clock with a workaholic boss. Before it veered further from the topic, it caught itself in time.

'In any case! What's important is that sales to earth have been absurdly low,' Bato said, unrolling a small scroll on the ground.

What was on the paper, which was now bigger than Bato itself, was surprisingly simple.

A bar chart. The horizontal axis was labelled *YEAR* and the set of bars got taller over time. Boreum glanced at the vertical axis – *SADNESS INDEX*.

'The sadness index hits a new high every year! Look, it broke the record again this year. Not that we didn't expect it to.'

Bato tapped on the chart several times, looking gloomy. As it said, this year's bar was the tallest.

'But! The problem is that the tears aren't selling! Logically speaking, sales should increase in proportion to the sadness index . . . I have absolutely no idea why humans aren't crying!'

Bato exclaimed as it wrung out the droplets from its dripping ears. When it shook its head, it was as if his confusion and sadness were spilling out from its ears.

'Everyone's blaming me. Well, the next-door department is fighting their own crisis. The happiness index has been dropping every year, but the demand for smiles remains ridiculously high. Isn't that terribly odd?'

Bo-reum thought about her life back on the moon. When she looked up, she'd see the blue lights from earth. Captivated by its brilliance, it was no surprise that she grew to have special feelings for the beautiful planet. But now that she was getting a much closer look, she realised that life on earth wasn't the beautiful azure she'd imagined.

Despite being miserable, people refused to cry and continued to plaster a smile on their faces when they were clearly unhappy. On earth, this phenomenon could be summarised in one phrase – *trying to fit in*.

For Bo-reum, choosing to stay on earth meant that in order not to stick out like a sore thumb, she had to do what everyone else did. At first, she found it odd, but with time, dissonance blunted into acceptance.

'Bo-reum-nim, do you know why people on earth are like this . . .?'

'Bato! Are you slacking over there? Get your butt here this instant!'

The two of them turned. A Tears Bunny was fixing its razor gaze on Bato. The huge scar running down its eyes made it looked even more intimidating.

'Eeks!'

Bato quickly pushed its name card into Bo-reum's hands.

'If you figure out the reason, please contact me! Promise!'

'Bato!'

At the thunderous roar of its boss, Bato burst into tears as it ran off. Bato's emotions had free rein on its face – whether it was the sadness, or the unhappiness of being wrongly accused. The rabbit had no qualms about showing how it truly felt, even when it was right in front of its boss. An odd sensation rose in Bo-reum. For a long while, she stood in the same spot, touching the name card.

Back at the shop, Bo-reum set down the heavy sack. When she glanced up, Mun was giving her a look that clearly said – *We're not done yet.*

'Are we still going somewhere?'

'Just one last place. The most important one.'

She sighed. But Mun, knowing that she'd come along, smiled.

He snapped his fingers, and a door appeared on the smooth wall.

The doorknob turned with a creak, and he stepped through lightly.

Trudging behind, Bo-reum sighed deeply, but it morphed into an exhale of awe as they emerged on the other side.

'Wow. This place's huge! I've never seen anywhere like this before.'

It was a library. Bookshelves were arranged at exact intervals as if someone had taken a measuring tape to them. Every single shelf was crammed tight with books.

Where does this end?

Bo-reum craned her neck, but the shelves seemed to stretch on infinitely.

'It's almost as if the books are alive.'

It was her first time here, but she felt strangely at home. She had the curious sensation that the books were whispering to her. One was singing a sweet tune, and from another, she heard the strong heartbeat of a brave knight. There were a couple that smelt like alcohol.

Among the books were stories of a young graduate's futile efforts to find a job; of an office worker who refused to give up on their dreams; of a child who was perpetually lethargic. Every book was glimmering, as if reminding everyone that there was no life that didn't contain at least one story.

'I used to be the custodian of this library. It was a rewarding experience.'

It was the first time Bo-reum had heard of this. Mun wasn't the type to share much about himself.

'So why did you quit?'

'To be precise, I was fired.' He made a gesture across his throat. 'I broke the rule that forbids us from interfering with the stories. Well, that's the conservative old fogeys for you. My younger brother has taken over as custodian.'

She chuckled as she thought about her own younger brother. Most of the time she found Mun impossible to understand, but today, she realised that they were similar in many ways. For one, they'd both left a job that they'd been doing for a long time.

Memories of her days as a guardian of the universe unfurled, inundating her with a wave of bitterness. To stop herself from spiralling further, she asked another question.

'So you're given free rein to the place even after you're fired? Good thing your sibling is the custodian now.'

She watched him stop in front of a shelf, take out a few books and leaf through them. Without tearing his eyes from the books, he replied, 'What are you talking about? Of course they won't give me permission. He's probably desperately searching for us now. And if we get caught, we'll have to close the shop.'

'Huh?!'

This was a serious confession, and yet he spoke to her with a carefree attitude as though he was discussing the weather. Thinking that it was his idea of a joke, she laughed drily. He flicked a glance at her and mirrored her laugh. *Ha ha.* A trail of tension sprung along her spine.

'Are you seriously telling me that we're trespassing? Come on, you're kidding, right?'

'These should be enough.'

Mun passed the armful of books to Bo-reum, and at that moment, a klaxon cut through the air, and red lights flashed.

'Aha. They got us.'

'*Aha, they got us?!*' Bo-reum shrieked. 'Oh no. What should we do now?'

'Without books, I can't make the cocktails, and if I can't make the cocktails, then I won't be able to pay you a salary. And isn't it better that these stories are being put to good use somewhere else instead of collecting dust on the shelves?'

She wanted to say something in retort, but the whole situation was so ridiculous that she was stumped for words.

Grrrrrng—

The security shutters were rolling down from the windows, shutting out the sunlight. Darkness was closing upon them. At this rate, something terrible might happen.

'Damn! What are you waiting for? The door!'

'No. If we pass through the door with these, we'll be caught for sure.'

'Then how?'

'We should pass through the stories.'

Bo-reum's brows were almost stitched together, while Mun was still happy to be leisurely browsing the shelves as though he couldn't hear the scary *thump, thump, thump* of heavy footsteps echoing down the hallway.

Finally, he seemed to have found the book he was looking for. He nodded and tapped it lightly against her forehead.

'I trust you'll do a good job.'

'Huh?'

It didn't make any sense at all. But before she could say anything, the book gleamed against her forehead.

Woosh!

Along with the pool of light, Bo-reum disappeared from the library. By the time the armed guards arrived at the spot, Mun, too, was nowhere in sight.

'Ahhh!'

Bo-reum screwed her eyes tight shut and hunched over in a protective position. However, the fear that someone might grab her at any moment suddenly vanished without a trace.

She cracked her eyes open. She was standing on a planet that was much smaller than the moon. Wrapped in her arms were the books Mun had passed her.

'How am I supposed to go back . . .?'

She scanned her surroundings, hoping to see a familiar constellation. But all around was darkness.

When did things start going wrong? When I quit being a guardian? When I left the moon for the earth? When I ended up in that strange shop?

Or was it the moment she met Mun? She let out a deep sigh that could fissure the ground. Suddenly, she felt a tap on her shoulder.

'Ah!'

'Oops, sorry. Didn't mean to scare you.'

Bo-reum spun around, clutching her chest, and her eyes met a familiar face. The fairy, who was taller than her peers, who held firm even when the others ridiculed her dream.

'Pamina?'

'It's been a long time!'

Pamina, Bo-reum; Bo-reum, Pamina. The two used to come as a pair, like what a thread is to a needle. Pamina was a fairy who yearned to be a guardian and Boreum was a strong rabbit who wanted to decorate the stars.

'It's been a long while,' Bo-reum returned the greeting.

The days of giggling and being the pillar of support for each other had faded into distant memories. Or rather, Bo-reum felt like a gap had opened up between them. Unlike her, Pamina had achieved her dream.

'What are you doing here? Are you lost?'

'Well, I . . .'

Pamina flashed her a grin, as if they were back in the old days. However, Bo-reum averted her gaze and lowered her head. An awkwardness hung in the air.

When Bo-reum left her job as a Moon Rabbit – that was a long time ago – she had to return the compass that helped her navigate her way in the universe. Pamina, having only heard from someone else that Bo-reum had quitted her job, didn't quite know what to say. But the one thing she was good at was directions.

'I see. Where do you want to go? I can take you there!'

Bo-reum wasn't very enthusiastic, but with no alternative in sight, she followed Pamina back to earth.

On the way, Pamina played the flute. The notes rang out beautifully and any stray meteorites that threatened to crash in their path made way for them. Bo-reum followed behind her silently until she found herself back at the shop entrance.

'Thank you, Pamina. If not for you, I'd be a lost child wandering around the universe.'

Today, the sign for the Moon Glow Bookshop looked a lot smaller than usual, and Bo-reum felt extra pathetic. She suppressed the lump of heat rising in her throat and flashed Pamina the brightest smile she could muster. Pamina, too, tried her best to ignore the awkward atmosphere.

'Bo-reum-ah, shall we hang out again soon? Like old times.'

Bo-reum smiled and nodded. 'Sure.'

Pamina clapped in delight. Because she had to return to her duties, the short reunion came to an end.

Bo-reum stood there and waved. For a long while after Pamina disappeared into the distance, she remained at the same spot, staring up at the sky.

A sigh escaped her.

Tinkle—

The door chime rang as she stepped inside the shop. The gentle glow of the lights greeted her, but today, the cosy space felt different from usual. Or rather, she didn't like it very much right now.

'You did well.'

When Bo-reum put down the stack of books, Mun greeted her in his usual relaxed manner. Irritation streaked through her, and she jabbed a finger at the wall clock.

'It's way past my working hours! I'm now a customer!' she snapped, sinking heavily into a chair.

In this moment, there was no employee and employer, just a customer and the bartender. Mun glanced at her, and seeing the sparks shooting from her eyes, the corner of his lips lifted.

'Welcome to the Moon Glow Bookshop. What would you like to have?'

Mun wore a smile, but it was not his usual playful grin. He was seriously treating her as a customer. Taking the menu, Boreum noticed that he had given her the one categorised by the backdrops of the stories.

She recalled what he'd said about the menus – *Grab whichever catches your eye. The right story will find its way to the customer.*

Bo-reum had no patience for the mood, experience or whatever it was he had in mind when he paired these drinks to the customer. She planned to pick a random drink, and when it was served, she'd take a sip and tell him, 'I don't think this cocktail suits me very well.'

'Hmm . . .'

She perused the menu, determined to choose one with the worst-sounding name. However, her gaze kept lingering on one of the drinks.

Mun, as though picking up on her dilemma, asked, 'Would you like to have that one?'

Her lips clamped tight. In the end, she gave a stiff jerk of her head.

'All right. One moment, please.'

Mun sliced the zesty lemon and added the sugar. At a couple of snaps of his fingers, the drink bubbled away, and on top, he sprinkled the blue powder as he did before.

'Your *Cosmos Fairy* is ready.'

It was the same drink that the young customer had ordered previously – the story of Pamina the fairy.

'This is the alcoholic version. Please enjoy the drink.'

The story of the tall fairy who wanted to be a guardian of the universe. Previously, Mun had lied that Pamina didn't manage to achieve her dreams. That was because in a non-alcoholic drink, he couldn't show the young girl the entire story.

But this time, once she finished the drink, she'd be able to know the truth. In her heart, a voice was screaming, *That's enough!* A part of her wanted to bolt out immediately, but the overwhelming curiosity lured her to reach for the glass.

How did Pamina end up being a guardian?

Bo-reum knocked back the cocktail.

'Only strong rabbits can become a guardian of the universe.'

With that, her dream shattered. With every utterance of that harsh truth, her heart grew as empty as the universe. *Should I give up?* she'd ask herself. That fateful day, she was also sobbing alone.

Shooting stars were falling like a waterfall in the night sky. Captivated by the mass migration of the stars, the fairies clapped and cheered. Only she gazed up at the meteor shower with sad eyes.

The falling stars reminded her of her dreams. No matter how she tried to cup her palms to catch them, they'd disappear in a second.

When the stars were gone, in its place, a new star would appear. After today, the inky sky would be filled with beautiful constellations once more. But knowing that wasn't enough to lift her spirits.

After the show, the fairies went back, and she was left alone. Then she saw it. A lone star in the sky. But its glow was so faint that if she didn't look closely enough, she'd have missed it.

Lured by the faint light, she came to a very small, shabby planet. It was so old that the ornaments the fairies had decorated it with were dated and worn out.

It'd probably disappear in no time, she thought. But there was something about the old shabby planet, and how nobody cared to take a second look at it that felt so relatable to her that she couldn't bear to leave it alone. In the end, she decided to spruce up the place.

She was sweeping all the loose pebbles into a corner when she heard a voice.

'You don't have to do this. I'm going to disappear soon.'

She looked around. There was no one. It was a while later that she realised the planet was speaking to her.

'I'm sorry to hear that.'

She continued sweeping. To exist means that one day, you will disappear. This is a fact of life, but because she was still young, her heart ached at the thought of it. The planet chuckled.

'There's nothing to be sorry for. It's a moment I've been waiting for.'

The girl couldn't understand. It didn't make sense that anyone, or anything, would look forward to disappearing from the world. Even if it was a planet that didn't shine as brightly as the others.

The old planet nodded, as if understanding her confusion.

'Many people look at the stars and make a wish. Especially the ones that shine brightly in the night sky. Unfortunately, I was never one of the bright ones.'

Every single word stabbed at her heart. It spoke calmly, but she could feel its sadness. The realisation that you were different, not because you were special, but because you couldn't match up to the rest. It was an indescribable despair. Pamina knew it all too well.

'Are you waiting for death?' she asked sadly.

'I'm not. My moment to shine will come. That I've been dimmer than the rest is because I'm still waiting to shine brighter than anyone else. And I can feel the moment approaching.'

The old planet's voice rang out stronger, louder. However, she couldn't share its excitement.

She thought of her grandma, who'd lied to her and given her false hopes. But she didn't want to show her disappointment, so she forced a nod and finished sweeping the ground.

'Thank you. I haven't felt so refreshed in a long time. In return, I'd love to give you a present. Take that box over there, will you?'

She turned. At the corner was a box. She wasn't very interested in it but thinking that it was probably the last present the planet could give someone, she nodded. Picking up the box, she bade the planet goodbye and then went on her way.

When she had gone far enough, she paused and opened it. Inside was a flute with holes carved into it.

But I don't know how to play the flute.

She was grateful for the present. However, it would most likely have gone into the storage room with the rest of her old toys, if not for the fact that she witnessed what was about to happen.

Vrrrr—!

Hearing a strange vibration, she whipped her head around. It came from where she'd just left. She held her breath as she watched the final moments of the old planet. In her heart, she prayed that the tiny, dim light could shine brightly for once.

However, its light only got dimmer. Watching the tiny dot flicker for what seemed to be the last time, tears spilled down her cheeks.

It was yet another lie.

She sniffed, sadness swirling in her eyes.

BANG—!

Pamina was momentarily blinded by the most dazzling light that filled her entire field of vision.

'Wow.'

Reflexively, she held out her palms to block out the strong rays and when her sight returned, her heart was still pounding.

'What was that?'

The white light stretched to fill the entire universe. At the centre of the flash was emptiness; she was sure that the old planet was there just moments ago.

'It wasn't a lie. No other stars could've matched your brilliance.'

The realisation shook her to her core, and for a while, enraptured by what she'd witnessed, she stood there, unable to move an inch.

It was as if the light also swept away the darkness in her heart. She thought about her dream again. And why she wanted to be a guardian of the universe.

You were right. You were bright, brighter than anyone else.

As she mulled over their conversation, something in the depths of her heart welled up, filling her. What the planet had given her wasn't just the gift of its beautiful light. Whenever she felt exhausted, she'd play the flute.

At first, she could barely blow a note. But she kept practising, and finally she could play an entire song. It was only then that she discovered its mysterious power.

The power to guide the meteorites that streaked across the universe. When she played her flute, everything – the meteorites, planets – was kept in order, and as a nod of acknowledgement to her powers, she finally became a guardian of the universe.

'Kyaaaa—'

A sweet scent spread from the tip of Bo-reum's nose. Because she drained the glass in one shot, the burn from the alcohol rose to the back of her throat in an instant.

She coughed and Mun poured her a glass of water, which she gulped down gratefully. When she put down the glass, she felt a little calmer.

'Another one?' Mun glanced at the empty cocktail glass.

She declined. Her head was starting to spin; she didn't think she could take another glass. How did the customers finish several cocktails?

She leaned forward and rested her heavy head that felt like a wet sponge onto the table. The sweetness had dissipated, leaving behind a tart dryness. Sour, just like how she was feeling.

'Loser . . .'

Pamina's story was like fantasy. Bo-reum should congratulate her, but she was a sore loser at heart; she didn't have it in her to feel genuinely happy for her friend.

Unlike Pamina, who chased her dream till the very end, Bo-reum gave up being a designer of the stars and joined the other strong rabbits to become a guardian and when she was assigned to look after the moon, she earned the title Moon Rabbit. Life couldn't always go according to her wishes, she told herself. It was the best she could do in those circumstances.

A dark shadow twisted itself in her heart, and it whispered to her: If she continued chasing after ideals, she was only going to fall behind. Because of that, she thought that one day, Pamina would also give up on her dreams and join the ranks of the other fairies.

Thinking back, the only person who had fallen behind was herself. Only she had yet to find her direction in life. She'd quit her job and came to earth to start afresh, but in reality, things weren't smooth sailing.

If only she could have a chance encounter like Pamina. Would that make all the difference? What if she met a muse to pull her out of her despair, received a gift that'd help her achieve her dreams? If she had been so lucky, would she have become a designer by now?

Despite her light-headedness, a heavy misery crawled all over her.

'Idiot! Stupid! Loser!'

She needed an outlet to let loose her frustrations. But she knew that these angry words would only boomerang back at her.

She glared at Mun, but he continued wiping a glass calmly.

'Shouldn't you at least comfort me?' she snapped.

Mun simply smiled. Crossing her arms, she stared at him, determined to wait it out until he said something.

He put down the glass and met her gaze. But before he said anything, the words tumbled out of her mouth.

'Did you know? Pamina and I are the same age. We're friends. When I passed the qualification test to be a guardian, do you know what I said to her?'

She rubbed her face in anguish as she thought back to what had happened, and the sadness etched on Pamina's face.

'*It's time to face reality. We aren't kids any more.* I told her that. Who was I to say that to her face? But I acted like I knew better. But look, luck is never on my side. See what I've become now – stealing from the library!'

With a sidelong scowl at the books, she sighed. Indeed, she was terribly unlucky. Unlike Pamina, who had received a precious gift from the planet, from the moment the Moon Rabbit arrived on earth, all she found was a bunch of people with a complete disregard for labour rights.

She worked hard at every job she had, only to end up getting taken advantage of. Because she didn't know better. Even right now, were things any different?

'There's a saying that people who are meant to succeed will find their way forward, but those who aren't can only remain where they were. I guess I am the latter.'

Acknowledging that aloud made her even more miserable. *I must be really drunk*, she thought. She forcibly swallowed the sobs that threatened to escape her mouth and rearranged her features in a semblance of calmness.

Guess I'm not the only one feeling this way.

People who refused to cry even when they were sad. That was why Bato couldn't make any sales. There were so many people out there who were just like her. Bo-reum sighed at the empty glass.

'Will my story have a happy ending?'

She knew that whatever Mun responded with wouldn't make a material difference. But even if it was just empty words, she wanted some comfort. However, Mun only gave her a one-word reply: 'Maybe?'

'That's mean,' she complained.

Mun didn't respond. Instead, he arranged several star-shaped handmade sweets on a patterned dish and placed them in front of her.

She cast an unenthusiastic glance at the dish. 'I didn't order this.'

'Consider it a thank you for helping me with the ingredients. You've worked hard.'

It was a kind gesture, but not one she could appreciate fully right now when she was in a bad mood. She couldn't bring herself to smile in return.

On the plate were seven bite-sized sweets in different colours, like a rainbow. Because they were so charmingly decorated, the sight of them cheered her up slightly.

'Stories can be based on happenings over several years or be completed by a day's events. In the stories of your life, there will be happy endings as well as sad ones.'

Mun was back to speaking in riddles. Keeping her flushed cheek splat on the table, Bo-reum stared at the sweets decorated in five colours.

'But when it comes to my dreams, it's been one sad ending after another. Maybe I should've stayed on the moon.'

'The ending is not determined by whether you achieved your dreams or not. It's shaped by your feelings and experiences. A sad ending is still possible when your dream has come true, ditto for the other way round.'

'Then what is considered a happy ending?'

For the first time, his expression shifted into a thoughtful look. The rest of the questions, he'd answered smoothly, but now, he moved his lips carefully, as if there was no real answer to the question.

'When you think back to something with little regret – perhaps that's a happy ending? Despite all the hardships, you still smile and say, *Ah, those were the days.*'

He arranged the clean glasses in a row before continuing.

'Regret sticks to us like a second shadow; it follows us wherever we go. But trying and failing will bring less regret than not trying at all. It's just like how people look back on their life and often lament that instead of being afraid, they should've at least tried. You're doing great.'

The moment flashed past in an instant, but the sincerity in his gentle voice touched Bo-reum.

She wasn't expecting a compliment at all. But hardened by the criticisms that everyone else had piled on her, even though a rush of warmth welled up in her, the words that escaped her lips were cold.

'So what if you tried? If you fail, everything becomes meaningless. I don't know what I'm doing any more. Am I really doing okay? Or should I live life the way others tell me to before it becomes too late? I have no idea. I'm sick and tired of sad endings all the time.'

'Have you heard of this saying? It's the coldest before spring, and the darkest before sunrise. People often talk about how the darkest moments come before success, so hang in there a little longer.'

The glasses arranged in a neat row flew back to their respective shelves.

Mun continued. 'But I think a little differently. Just like how spring follows winter, darkness and light touch each other, success and failure aren't too different.'

'How are they not different? Failure is misery, success is happiness!'

Bo-reum's speech was slurring. Mun smiled.

'If success is what fills the heart, then failure is what strengthens it. Personally, instead of success stories, I prefer stories about growth and resilience.'

'You're just saying this to comfort me.'

'I'm not. Didn't I say it before? My favourite scenes in fairy tales are the bits before the happily-ever-after, when the protagonist is living in the anxiety of not knowing what's ahead. The way that they keep going forward despite the odds makes me feel big feelings. And I find myself rooting for them from the bottom of my heart.'

Noticing her doubtful expression, he whispered conspiratorially, 'That's why I was fired from my custodian job. I wasn't supposed to intervene with the stories, but how could I resist the desire to be their cheerleader?'

'Puhahaha.'

Bo-reum burst into laughter. Hearing about his recklessness seemed to relieve that dull ache in her heart.

'I'm also cheering for you. Things are probably going to be tough. At times, the future may seem so bleak that the road ahead feels like a thick fog. Who knows? Maybe you might even end up failing. Despite everything, I'm rooting for you. You're amazing. Whether you're doing what you do because you want to, or because you don't have a choice. The fact that you didn't give up and kept going reminds me of the stars in the night sky – you're shining just as brightly.'

Mun held his gaze steady. Until a moment ago, Bo-reum was still chortling, but now, she scratched her ears in embarrassment.

'Oh, come on,' she muttered.

Catching himself, Mun bounced back to his usual expression.

Slightly pink in the face, Bo-reum picked up a sweet from the dish and bit into it. A rush of sugary goodness filled her mouth, and the corners of her lips lifted.

'How is it? I made it with the ingredients we bought today.'

She nodded. 'Delicious.'

The more she chewed, the deeper the aroma seemed to envelope her senses.

She munched happily, and her eyes met Mun's, whose playful glint was back. Leaning forward, he rested his chin on his palms and asked, 'How delicious is it?'

It was the expression he had when he occasionally asked her for comments about his cocktails. If she gave him a generic response, he'd pick apart her words and launch into a barrage of questions until he was satisfied.

Bo-reum swallowed the last bite and thought about it. Then the answer came to her.

'It makes my day end on a good note.'

Chapter 5
Jewel Fairy

Today was the fifth day of the month. It was an ordinary morning just like any other, but to Bo-reum, today was a special day. She wiped the tables with more diligence, dusted even the most obscure corners of the shop that she'd usually ignore. And the whole time, her gaze never once left Mun.

'Bo-reum-ah.'

The moment Mun raised his head, she teleported to him right away.

'Thank you for all your hard work this past month.'

Bo-reum broke into a grin as she took the money envelope. It was thicker than the previous month, thanks to the special clause in her contract. It looked like the internet sales were doing well.

'You sure it's okay for me to have the bonus? I haven't done anything to help you on the online sales,' Bo-reum asked with an apologetic glance at him.

But as she spoke, she held on tightly to the envelope. It didn't look like she'd be willing to return the money to him either way. Mun chuckled.

'You did. I saved quite a bit on the delivery fees, and I didn't have to wait for the ingredients. You also helped to taste-test some of the drinks sold online.'

She nodded vigorously.

Oh yes. That's hard work.

Plus, her shoulders had almost dislocated under the weight of Mun's shopping. And thinking back to the close shave at the library and how she almost became a lost and wandering girl in the universe, she deserved every single cent of the bonus.

Yay!

Her eyes lit up when she peeked into the envelope.

'But I took away the cost of the cocktail you drank.'

Her expression froze. But the next second, she nodded and bounced back to her happy face.

Oh well, I was the one who wanted a drink.

She had insisted on being a customer that day. It was only right that she paid for it, but she was curious how much it was.

As if anticipating her question, Mun added, 'Ninety per cent of your bonus.'

'Huhhhhhh?'

She hurriedly checked the money in the envelope. The wad of notes was much thicker than usual, so she could immediately estimate how much the original bonus was. Her jaw dropped.

Her bonus, if she'd gotten it in full, was higher than her monthly pay. In other words, she drank a month's worth of pay in one glass.

'That's too expensive!'

Bo-reum's face crumpled. *What a rip off!* With a sideways glance at her, Mun spoke, a solemn expression in his eyes.

'How could I skimp on the ingredients when you were my special customer? I gave you the royal treatment.'

'Didn't you say that I was doing great? That you'll be rooting for me? You said so many nice, encouraging words. You could've also given me a discount . . .'

'Well, you said you wanted to be treated like a customer. Now, you're my staff,' Mun said in a business-like tone.

A playful smile tugged on his lips. She knew it. He was doing it on purpose!

Bo-reum wanted to scream, but she swallowed her anger with difficulty. The only silver lining was that the bonus was unbelievably good. She had no idea how fast the online drinks were flying off the shelves, but she hoped that it'd be the same next month. And never ever would she ask for a cocktail from Mun. Never!

Tinkle—

Having gotten a taste of the bonus, Bo-reum's eyes gleamed red and she hurried to greet the customer at the door.

'Welcome to the Moon Glow Bookshop—' she called out, but paused midway.

The customer had not entered from the main entrance, but a side door.

'Hello.'

A shoulder-length bob framed her young face. It wasn't just her face that was young. She was wearing a school uniform.

'May I know how old you are?'

Bo-reum was just trying to stall for time. She shot Mun a meaningful look, hoping he'd get the hint to do something about the alcohol bottles lining the shelves.

'Our shop doesn't serve under-aged—'

'I know what this shop sells, Bo-reum . . . nim.'

It looked like the young girl wasn't quite sure how to address her politely, so she hesitated before tacking on the polite 'nim' at the end. In school, she probably didn't have many chances to meet someone whom she'd need to call '-ssi' or '-nim'.

But that wasn't the point. The girl was obviously looking at her name tag, which spelt out *MOON RABBIT*. Yet, she had called her 'Bo-reum'.

'Manager Mun.'

Bo-reum called out to Mun, a confused look on her face. He waved them over, so the young girl followed Bo-reum to the counter, where she sat opposite him.

Mun tapped on his name tag. 'Can you read what's on it?'

'Moon,' she said. 'In the sky.'

This was the first time Bo-reum heard a customer answer his question this way. Usually, they'd see *MUN* and think of the Korean word for 'door'. No one had ever called him 'Moon'.

She recalled what he'd said to her when he gave her the name tag. That if a customer called her Bo-reum instead of Moon Rabbit, she needed to be careful.

He had told her this so solemnly; the same way one would warn others against falling for a phishing scam.

'This is the place that sells special drinks, right?'

Bo-reum felt a trail of goosebumps on her arms. The young girl knew exactly what the shop was.

Back then, she'd asked Mun what would happen if they accepted a customer who could read their name tags differently. 'We'll be dragged away,' was his answer. He didn't sound like he was joking, and she gulped hard, imagining this customer to be a gruesome monster of some sort. Never in her wildest imagination did she think that the customer who posed such a threat to their shop, who would read their name tags differently, would be a teenage girl.

He offered her his usual smile. 'That's right, dear customer.'

The girl heaved a sigh of relief. Ever since she bought that drink on the internet, she had gone through so much.

'You can't imagine how hard I've been searching for your shop.'

'You're actually quite lucky to be able to find it.'

At his words, the frustrations that she'd held in threatened to bubble up and spill over. One day, she'd come across a website selling drinks, and even though she usually didn't like flavoured drinks, the colours were so gorgeous that she couldn't help but order one to try – the only non-alcoholic option.

And given what had happened afterwards, she quickly returned to the site only to break out in a cold sweat at the words 'SOLD OUT'. She was desperate to know when the drink would be restocked, but there was no phone number or address.

'Hmm?' A soft murmur escaped her.

That was strange. *Without an address or phone number, how did I manage to make my way here?* But when her eyes met Mun's, she remembered what she was here for.

'When will it be restocked?' she asked, her voice tinged with urgency. 'The blue drink with yellow layers.'

'Aha. You must be looking for the sparkling water – *Bubbles of Calmness*. Oh dear. I have no plans to make more anytime soon.'

The girl turned an ashen grey. She stood up so abruptly that Bo-reum jumped. Mun's ominous warning rang in her head, and she tensed up.

'Please, I beg of you. Even if it's just one bottle. I really need it next week.'

The girl's name was Jung Sohee. She was running for the school president, and elections were just around the corner. Everyone, from her form teacher to her classmates, were giving her their fullest support; her friends helped to come up with ideas for her campaign pledges and stayed up late with her to make posters.

However, she couldn't stop worrying. Her rival was a star athlete in school, and extremely popular. He was rumoured to come from a wealthy family and already, his posters were more polished and professional than hers.

'I'm sorry,' Mun said. 'I have no plans to make more, and in any case, our policy is to sell only one drink to under-aged customers.'

A crack of anxiety bellowed in her heart. But when she was on the site, she didn't recall having to verify her identity or age. If only she'd had the sense to purchase a few more when she was placing her original order . . . it made sense to her that it was now all sold out.

Regret rained down on her like a crushing downpour.

'Please. I have to give a speech next week. I'm going to screw up without the drink.'

What she was afraid of wasn't her rival's family background or his charisma, but herself. She was scared that she couldn't do it.

'When I stand in front of others, my heart feels like it's going to burst. I didn't used to have stage fright, but now . . . I have no idea what to do.'

On election day, she'd be giving a speech in front of the whole student body. In the past, she never had problems presenting her ideas logically and calmly, but at some point, she grew to be afraid of the many pairs of eyes staring at her. Her legs would tremble, her forehead beaded with sweat. It was hard for her to accept the abrupt changes in herself. She'd thought it temporary, but her symptoms never got better.

Bo-reum piped up. 'How about taking a Cheongsimhwan? The herbal pill might help you relax.'

Sohee shook her head and sighed.

'It doesn't work for me. It only makes me very sleepy, and I can't focus.'

Her anxious eyes returned to Mun. Placing her palms together, she pleaded.

'But your drink was great. I breezed through my music performance test. No side effects either.'

However, the effects didn't last long. After a trip to the toilet, her anxiety returned.

'Please, I beg you. Just one more bottle.'

Sohee was close to tears. Mun could feel Bo-reum's intense gaze. It looked like she was on the girl's side.

Just one bottle. Isn't it okay? – her eyes seemed to be asking.

Arms folded, Mun looked at both of them in turn. Then he flashed his signature impish grin.

'Well, I have no plans to make more *Bubbles of Calmness*. But I have some of the concentrate left – it's the key ingredient. I suppose I can sell that to you.'

Bo-reum couldn't shake off a vague sense of unease. However, Sohee's face brightened noticeably, relief etched on her features.

'Would you like the concentrate? But it's going to be expensive . . .'

Sohee fumbled with her purse nervously. Behind her,

Bo-reum was reminded of how she'd been ripped off by him. If he dared ask for an exorbitant sum, she wasn't going to let him off the hook this time.

'Here you go, and I'll throw in two for free. The night before, mix it in water and drink it,' Mun said as he placed three rectangular glass bottles on the table.

Sohee stared at the blue liquid undulating in the bottles and swallowed hard.

'How much is it . . .?'

'You can pay for it later.'

Mun placed both hands on the edge of the table and leaned forward slightly in a bow.

That's illegal!

Because Sohee had her back towards her, she didn't notice Bo-reum glaring hard at Mun. Looking at the bottles, Sohee nodded.

'Thank you.'

Mun smiled. Before Bo-reum could say anything, Sohee swept the bottles into her arms and scurried off out of the store. The side door creaked as it closed.

'She's still so young, *tsk*.'

Sohee stirred awake to find herself lying on a bench. Was it all a dream? She propped her stiff body up and looked around. A few residents passing by were giving her dirty stares. She recalled coming to the park because she was so frustrated. She'd sat down hoping to take a short rest, and it looked like she'd fallen asleep.

She sighed. Suddenly, her fingers brushed against something cold. It was a bottle with blue liquid.

'So, it wasn't a dream!'

Clutching the bottles close to her, Sohee looked up. Above her, the full moon was glowing.

She squealed inwardly. Fearing that the bottles might suddenly vanish, she quickly carried them home.

'I'm back!'

To avoid her mum's unnecessary questions, she quickly went to the fridge, grabbed herself a bottle of water, returned to her room and hid herself under the blankets. She could breathe easy again, as if something that had weighed heavily on her had been lifted.

Eager to test out the effects as soon as possible, she poured out a glass of water and reached for one of the blue bottles.

Plonk. The fragrance of the ocean burst out immediately when the cork was pulled out. Tilting the bottle over the glass of water, she watched as the blue concentrate began to dissolve in beautiful blue swirls in the water like an abstract painting.

'Huu—'

Sohee sat down on the bed, and gulped down the drink.

She closed her eyes tentatively, but she didn't feel any difference. Looking doubtful, she was about to get up when a wave of drowsiness hit her.

Forgetting that she hadn't even brushed her teeth, she slipped into a deep sleep.

The next morning, in class, an opportunity to verify the effectiveness of the drink came up.

'Today's date is . . . All right, Student 19, come up to the board and solve this question,' said the teacher with salt-and-pepper hair as he glanced at the calendar.

Sohee's student number was 19. She pushed back her chair

and slowly made her way to the chalkboard at the front of the classroom.

'Excellent!'

A smatter of applause spread through the room. All eyes were on her. Yet she wasn't trembling. Like in the past, she gave a relaxed smile. Her heart wasn't threatening to burst out of her chest, neither did her legs wobble like jelly.

'Wait. You got over your stage fright?' Right after class, her best friend sidled up to her. Yoon Yeji, who had suggested that she run for school president, was her right-hand woman for the campaign and the friend most concerned about her sudden bout of stage fright. She breathed out a sigh of relief. 'That's great!'

It was truly a relief. Sohee nodded happily. That afternoon, after finishing their prep work for the election, she and her friends headed to a tteokbokki snack shop.

'I knew you'd get better in no time. Cos you aren't just any Sohee, but my best friend Jung Sohee!' Yeji exclaimed as she speared a rice cake with her fork.

'What do you mean? You were the most worried,' another friend teased, chuckling.

'Who? Not me!'

They spent the entire afternoon chatting and laughing. How long had it been since she'd felt so relaxed? Sohee wondered to herself.

Why was I so anxious all the time?

Ever since her symptoms had worsened, Sohee found it hard to laugh even when she was with her friends. But not today. She was so relaxed that she was starting to doubt that her symptoms had really ever been that bad. Perhaps after today, she was now cured completely.

Feeling hopeful, she slept well that night. Not knowing that the effects of the blue drink were slowly fading like fumes dissipating into the sky.

Ruby was a wingless fairy, round and small like a baseball, her body as red as the ripest of apples. She looked around but the rest of the fairies were nowhere in sight. She'd ignored the rule not to break rank, and in her greed to dig and devour a jewel, she was left behind. However, it didn't matter. Ruby was strong.

Ruby stuck her legs into the ground and used her strong hands to dig. Her gaze was so fierce and determined that even the animals didn't dare come near. Not the tiger, not the bear. The only one who came up to Ruby was a curious human.

'You're amazing!'

Ruby couldn't understand the human's language. '*Ge-ru-ruk!*' she cried out. Any other animal would've put its tail between its legs and backed off. But the human creased his brows and smiled.

Seeing that the human wasn't scared of her, something indescribable sprouted in her heart. No matter how much she shouted at the human, he didn't leave. Her cries were loud and shrill, but the human simply wore earplugs and remained by her side.

'Should I help?'

The human imitated what Ruby did. But instead of using his hands, he brought a pickaxe that was much bigger in size compared to her hands. Looking at the human as he followed her actions, she felt an odd sense of kinship.

'Ha—'

Sohee woke up gasping for air, her heart pounding in her

chest. Were the effects of the drink wearing off? But she wasn't standing in front of a crowd right now. She was in bed.

Have my symptoms worsened?

At a loss for what to do next, she curled up in bed, shaking uncontrollably. She heard her mother waking her up, but choked by her own breath, she couldn't answer her calls. Finding the prolonged silence to be strange, her mum hurried into her room only to find her drenched in cold sweat.

'Sohee-ya!'

In her mum's embrace, Sohee's pounding heart seemed to ease a little. And with the tension slipping away, the tears began to fall.

'Mum, I want to stay at home and rest.'

She could barely eke out the words between sobs. Her mum stroked her hair and nodded. This was the first time in her life that she was absent from school. And of all days, it was Friday, the last campaign day before next week's elections.

On such an important day . . .

She lay in bed the whole day. Several times, she thought of getting up and going to school, but her heart started pounding wildly again, and she could only retreat under the blanket even further.

She felt a nagging guilt about her friends who were helping her and only wanted the best for her. For the entire day, her phone buzzed with missed calls and messages, but she didn't touch it.

She imagined her friends at the tteokbokki snack shop glaring at her with cold eyes. Despite summoning all her strength to shake it off, the image took root in her mind.

They must be so disappointed.

She imagined their scornful expressions, and Yeji shaking

her finger at her. Sohee knew it was all in her head, but it didn't make the torment any less.

I can't take it any more.

Sohee quickly poured out a glass of water from the jug on her bedside table. She popped open another bottle and watch as the blue concentrate diffused into the clear water.

Gulp, gulp. She downed the entire glass, and all the anxiety slipped out of her as if it'd never happened, and she fell into a deep sleep.

Like any other day, Ruby was digging with her tiny hands. Next to her, the human was doing the same with the pickaxe. Ruby bounced up to the man who was sweating profusely.

'Ggi-e-ekk!'

In her hand she held out a shiny jewel. It was the leftover from what she was eating. Out of pity for the man, who was raining buckets of sweat, she held it out to him. He must be hungry. She didn't mind sharing her food with him.

'You're giving it to me?'

The man held up the jewel to the light for a while, seemingly drunk in its glory. Looking at his wide grin, Ruby was delighted. From then on, they fell into the habit of helping each other.

Ruby had a great nose for sniffing out where the jewels were, and once she waved her tiny arm, the man would dig with his pickaxe.

'Please do your best today, too.'

The man's appetite was getting bigger by the day. Ruby would eat her fill before giving the rest of the day's jewels to the man. Once, she saw him putting them into his pocket, and she immediately thought the pocket was his mouth. But over time his mouth kept growing bigger, and in no time, it was as big as a sack.

'You're amazing!' the man exclaimed.

Ruby didn't have to eat jewels every day. However, because the man kept coming to look for them, she had no choice but to go with him. Despite knowing the rule that over-harvesting jewels was forbidden, her heart softened at the sight of his happy face.

'Good to know you, kiddo.'

As time passed, more and more people came to find Ruby. Everyone was lovely to her. They called her the Jewel Fairy. She was welcomed with opened arms and while she wasn't quite used to it, she didn't dislike that feeling.

'How pretty you are today, Jewel Fairy.'

Every day they came, and it felt like life would go on for ever like this. However, that wasn't to be.

'We're moving on to a different place. It's been great knowing you, kiddo.'

One by one, the people started to leave. The ground was now barren. Everyone else had a place to go, but not Ruby. Left behind, she tried digging for jewels but there were none left.

'Be well, Jewel Fairy.'

With the last person gone, Ruby was left alone. The sun went down, and darkness descended, but nobody came to find her. No matter how hard she dug, there was no sight of a jewel. Not even a glimmer. The ground was full of holes. Hunger gnawed at her, and one day, she could no longer move.

'*Ggi-e-ekk*,' she cried out. It wasn't the extreme hunger, but the vast emptiness in her heart that crushed her.

Why did I even help them? What was it that I truly wanted?

Ruby's sight narrowed to a tunnel, and finally, her last wisp of strength gave way to darkness.

What a strange dream.

Rays of light filtered through the gaps in the curtains as Sohee rubbed her eyes and got up. *Thump, thump.* Her heart was beating normally, and on the ground, her legs weren't shaking. It looked like she was back to her usual self.

Only one left.

Out of the three bottles on her table, two were empty.

I need to do something.

She'd have to keep the last one for Monday – election day. The problem was Sunday. If the effects wore off, she'd be buried in the anxiety for an entire day.

She quickly got ready to head out. She would go back to that shop again. If the extreme anxiety she was feeling was a side effect from the drinks, she'd demand compensation. It didn't even come with a warning label!

'Ah.'

Before that, she had something else to do. On her phone screen was a long list of missed calls and message notifications. Her friends must be worried sick.

The first person she called was Yeji.

'Are you okay?' Yeji asked the moment the call connected. After making sure that she was fine, Yeji updated her about the random happenings in school yesterday. At the thought that her friends were working so hard to help her with her campaign, Sohee felt a rush of gratitude and guilt.

'We're meeting today, right? But don't push yourself. Only if you feel well enough . . .' Yeji tried to keep her tone light.

'Yes, I'll be there!'

Sohee suddenly remembered that they were planning to hang out today, after the campaign ended yesterday.

She glanced at the clock. If she didn't want to be late, she'd better hurry up. 'See you later,' she said before hanging up.

Sohee deliberately greeted her mum with a brighter voice than usual. Her mum scanned her with worried eyes, but seeing that she had returned to her regular self, she looked relieved.

'Mum, I'm heading out now.'

Outside, the warm sunshine and birds chirping seemed to hold her anxiety at bay. Sohee was relieved that she could smile as usual to her friends.

'Jung Sohee! Do you know how worried we were?' They all ran up to Sohee, their eyes reflecting genuine worry.

I have such great friends, what exactly am I afraid of?

For the sake of her friends, she made up her mind that she'd deliver a perfect speech next week.

'I'm hungry. What should we eat?'

It'd only been a day away from her friends, but she felt a rush of affection seeing them again. Time passed by quickly. They ate pizza, then belted out their favourite songs at the *noraebang* before going to a café to soothe their hoarse throats.

'Sohee, you want a vanilla latte too, right?' Yeji asked.

She nodded. They'd chosen a popular café known for its aesthetics, but luckily, they managed to get a table just as a group vacated it.

Everything was going well today, and she was in a good mood. Just as the drinks arrived, one of their friends tossed out a casual question and Sohee felt something catch in her throat.

'Hmm?'

Sohee looked up, doing her best to hide her fluster. That friend was a transfer student and she'd known her for a shorter period than the others.

'What is it that you really like?'

It didn't seem like the friend was intentionally aggressive. Seeing how Sohee was staring, the friend scratched her head awkwardly.

'I mean, everyone else will sometimes suggest eating something or going somewhere, but you seem to be okay with anything. And even your coffee order. You always get the same as Yeji.'

Vanilla latte. Indeed, she'd gone along with what Yeji had chosen.

Have I always liked vanilla lattes?

It was as if by asking the question, the friend had thrown a stone into a still river. Just last night, she had the sparkling water of calmness. Yet now, a queasy anxiety was starting to wriggle in the corner of her heart. She was unnerved.

'That's just Sohee being considerate,' said Yeji.

Despite her good friend's attempt to relieve the tension, her expression remained stiff.

The friend who asked the question immediately looked sorry for making the atmosphere awkward. In a valiant attempt to save the conversation, she tried switching topics.

'I heard you performed in a school play during your middle-school field trip.'

Yeji's eyes widened as she whipped her head around. The friend realised, belatedly, that she had asked another taboo question. Just as everyone was visibly struggling to find something appropriate to say, Sohee spoke.

'I did. But I forgot my lines and ruined it.'

Yeji was casting anxious glances at her, but Sohee answered as though it didn't matter. 'Thinking of it still gives me the shivers.'

Sohee chuckled, and almost immediately, the atmosphere warmed considerably. Only Yeji was looking at Sohee with a confused expression. She had been there that day and seen at first hand how much it had affected Sohee and how she'd bawled the entire day.

Sohee continued. 'I should've—'

Thud—!

She dropped the cup she was holding, spilling its contents across the table and creating a huge mess. There was a commotion of scraping chairs as everyone scrambled to get up.

'Hey, are you okay?'

'Oh, sorry. I'm okay. Yeah, it's fine. I'm so sorry. My bad.'

Unlike her friends who were flustered, Sohee remained collected, even when the hot drink spilt onto her leg. Or rather, she was smiling as though she couldn't feel anything. Like a robot.

Sohee went to the toilet to wash her hands. Nobody saw her hands tremble slightly.

'Today was fun!'

After leaving the café, they went to the arcade and later, they watched a movie. Sohee was all smiles and chatter, but the images of how she'd ruined the afternoon loomed in her mind. The moment they bade each other goodbye, she dropped the forced lift of her lips.

'I'm back.'

Stepping through the front door, Sohee plastered the smile back on her face. This time for the sake of her parents, who had been worried about her since yesterday. As for the soggy dregs that were her feelings, she tried to shove them further down and into a corner.

'Dad bought fried chicken.'

At the delicious aroma, she gulped down her saliva. Her parents and younger brother were already at the table waiting for her. Sohee quickly washed her hands and joined them.

The TV was airing a talk show, and the audience were laughing. Feeling her parents' eyes on her, Sohee put in extra effort to look at ease as she tore off a piece of chicken.

'Sohee-ah, don't worry so much.' When the first of the two chickens was reduced to bones, her dad spoke encouragingly. Her mother must've told him that she was having a hard time because of her upcoming election speech. 'You'll do fine. I have faith in you,' he added, and her mum murmured an agreement.

Her brother gave her a sideways glance. 'Well, do your best.'

The warm looks should've energised her. Instead, nausea climbed up her spine and she resisted the overwhelming desire to retch. Holding her breath, she smiled and nodded.

'Oh, my friend is here. She's helping me with the campaign. I'll head out for a bit to meet her.'

Sohee made a show of checking her phone and fled out of the house. Another moment longer and her legs would've given way. All she could think of was to escape.

Panting, she ran to the park near her house. With difficulty, she lowered herself onto a bench and stared down at her trembling legs.

Are the effects wearing off?

The last blue drink bottle was at home. But even if she had it with her now, she couldn't drink it. She had to save it for her speech.

Stop, stop!

No matter how hard she screamed in her head, her dreaded memories refused to budge. They only grew clearer, sharper.

Back in middle school, their form teacher, who was new and overzealous, had suggested that they prepare a play to perform on the last night of the upcoming field trip. The class responded enthusiastically; everything was going fine until the classmate playing the female lead had appendicitis and pulled out at the last minute.

In the scramble for a substitute, Sohee's name came up. Being the type who could never say no, she found herself roped in without quite knowing what was happening. She went with the flow, thinking that she'd be fine.

Was it because she had less time to practise? On that fateful day, she froze on the stage for the first time. Her mind was a complete blank; she couldn't remember any of the lines. Her constant mistakes turned the entire play into a fiasco. Everyone's eyes seemed to bore into her; time slowed to a standstill. Everything was going wrong. Hearing the laughter mixed with scorn, Sohee felt the world closing in on her.

Stop! That's enough!

The fear that she thought she'd forgotten threatened to inundate her again.

'What are you doing here?'

Just as darkness was about to swallow her up, a voice rang out next to her. She looked up to see a sweat-glistened face. Of all the people she could bump into, it was her rival in the election.

'Park Ji-ung . . . ?'

'Are you okay? You don't look well.'

Sohee quickly turned away. She didn't want him to see this side of her. She tried to compose herself, but her lips wouldn't stop trembling.

'Oh. I had a nightmare.'

Sohee winced at the lame excuse. But she struggled to think of something else. She kept her head down but didn't hear him leaving.

'Hmm.'

After a short pause, he broke the silence.

'What did you dream of?'

'Never mind.'

'Tell me. If you talk about it, you might feel better.'

Sohee was a little pissed off at his persistence. She had enough on her plate as it was. However, she couldn't show her annoyance. Because she was supposed to be the friendly and warm Sohee. Because she was the considerate friend, who never had anywhere she particularly wanted to go or anything she wanted to eat, always happy to go along with what others wanted.

'Well. Um. I dreamt that I was a fairy who eats jewels. Then I met a human and told him where to find all the jewels and I stupidly didn't leave any for myself.'

'That sounds so like you.'

'What?!'

Do you even know me?!

She jutted out her chin angrily.

'Well, you never seem to be able to say no to others. If you were the fairy, I believe you'd have told those people where the jewels are.'

Now that she was looking up at him, she realised that he was carrying a big squarish bag. On the side, written in big letters, were the words: SPEED DELIVERY.

'What's that?'

'Isn't it obvious? A delivery bag. I'm doing my part-time job now.'

'You work part-time? What for? Isn't your family rich? You must get given a lot of allowance already . . . and I saw your election posters!'

Ji-ung frowned and shrugged.

'Oh please, not at all. Those are all rumours. I earn my own allowance. And I paid for those posters with the money from my part-time job.'

Rumours?

She couldn't bring herself to accept that everything she'd been jealous of was the result of his hard work. A ripple of resentment ran through her, and her next words came out with a hardened edge.

'Get on with your work then. Stop hovering.'

'I'm just concerned; do you have to talk to me this way? I remembered how you'd cried back then, so I just wanted to make sure you're okay.'

Ji-ung attended the same middle school; they were even in the same class. After she messed up the entire play, she became known as the girl who forgot her lines. As always, a fiasco got more attention than success.

Her classmates back then all got front-row seats to her embarrassment.

'I'm going to screw this one up, too.'

Looking at her ex-classmate brought back even more vivid memories of that school trip. She lowered her head and heard him sigh.

'If you really don't want to do it, then withdraw. I'll be the school president.'

'How can I drop out? My friends have put so much effort into this!'

She couldn't help but raise her voice. How long had it been

since she last showed her anger towards someone? In between her sharp breaths, she still looked up to check if he was hurt by her outburst.

Ji-ung was nonchalant. 'Tell me. Why do you want the role?'

Sohee pursed her lips into a thin line. *Why do I want to be president?* Because her best friend suggested it.

Not just Yeji. Her teachers, her classmates were supportive too. She didn't want to disappoint them. Was this yet another vanilla latte? Had she ordered it only because others liked it, and she was just fine with it? Did she really like it? She wasn't quite sure.

Sohee turned the question back at Ji-ung. 'Then what about you? Why do you want to be the school president?'

He didn't hesitate a beat. 'I want to build a football field. That's my campaign pledge. I'll propose the idea to the school if I become the school president.'

Ji-ung loved football. While it was debatable if he was doing this for himself or for the students, his answer was so straightforward that she couldn't help but chuckle.

'If you really don't want to do this, withdraw.'

'Oh please. How can I do that?'

Her mood dampened. Ji-ung put down his bag and sat next to her.

'Why not? If you don't want to do it, just say it.'

Sohee imagined herself doing that. Telling everyone on election day that she wanted to give up. The horrified looks on her friends' faces morphing into the same expression her form teacher had worn during the field trip. In the audience, the rest of the students jeered and pointed fingers at her.

'No, I can't do it. What's everyone going to say!'

'No one is that interested in you. Even if they are, they only see what they want to. Look at me. A rich kid, did you say?'

He nudged the delivery bag with his foot.

'But my friends . . .'

'You feel sorry for them? So sorry you're forcing yourself to do what you don't want to? Oh please, as if they'd be happy to watch you do that.'

What Ji-ung said wasn't wrong, but she couldn't bear to single-handedly ruin their expectations. If she did, it felt as if her friends' attitudes towards her would change. Just like the teacher who had suggested that she took over the lead role.

'It doesn't matter if they're your family or friends. Or that they only have good intentions and want the best for you. If you don't like something, then it's not for you. Or are you going to live your entire life listening to everyone else?'

Suddenly, she thought of the jewel fairy. Ruby, who was left all alone in the end. Helping humans shouldn't have been a bad thing, but it made her lose her own home.

At the beginning, the jewel fairy was confident. No matter what obstacles she faced, she'd get through them. But when everyone eventually left her, she sank into a deep slump, unmotivated to get up, much less find a new home. Perhaps what she dug out from the ground wasn't jewels, but pieces of her true self.

What is it that I really want? Sohee asked herself the same question.

'Instead of going through with something you might regret in the future, listen to your heart.'

Sohee thought Ji-ung was rather like an adult. She had only ever seen him play football at lunchtimes, but he appeared much more observant and considerate than she had given him credit for.

'Don't keep putting others before yourself. Be true to yourself and live life alongside your loved ones.'

'You sound like you've seen everything in life.'

'I'm a deep thinker. Don't you think that makes me the best qualified to be a school president?'

Sohee burst out laughing. He grinned.

She glanced at his delivery bag. 'Don't you have to return to work?'

'I just finished delivering pizza nearby – that was my last job. I'm done for the day.'

Sohee was grateful for the chance encounter. Talking to him had made the debilitating anxiety fade considerably.

'Admit it. You like me, don't you?' Sohee joked.

Ji-ung looked aghast. 'Oh, please.'

Sohee chortled. In the past, she'd never have dared to make such a joke. She'd be horrified to even imagine what the other person would think of her.

But now that she said it aloud, it felt as though all her worries were for nothing.

He'd seen her at her worst. And perhaps because of that, she felt more at ease. That way, he wouldn't have any expectations of her.

'Okay, I got to go.'

The anxiety no longer pressed down on her, as if she'd just drank a whole glass of the sparkling water of calmness. Sohee looked up at the sky, at the full moon glowing above.

Monday arrived. The candidates gave their speeches, and the students voted. Park Ji-ung, the newly elected school president, went up on stage and reiterated his promise to build a football field.

'Ahhh. If only!'

Yeji poked their friend before glancing at Sohee. Sohee knew that her best friend was being considerate of her feelings, but she wasn't the least bit disappointed. Because it was all part of her plan.

The last bottle stood untouched on the table. With the full intent to mess up her speech, the pressure that had weighed on her had disappeared completely.

Instead of pretending that she was fine when she wasn't, the other way round was much easier. She was good at acting; that was why she was chosen as a substitute that time. When she was giving her speech, she pretended to fumble, keeping up with that unconfident act right until the voting ended. Come to think of it, she was *really* good at acting.

'I'm okay.'

This time, it came from her heart. She was truly okay. However, Yeji was close to tears as she hugged her. Everyone's efforts went down the drain because of her. Yet, she was the one being comforted. Sohee felt a warmth spread in her chest.

'Please hand in your forms for the special activity.' When they returned to class, the room was a flurry of chatter and movement. Next week, they were having special classes and there was a list to choose from.

'Sohee-ya, you're also joining the movie club, right?'

Because all the participants needed to do was to watch movies, it was a popular choice among the students. All her friends were keen to go for that. Sohee perused the list. Just as Yeji was about to go forward to hand in her form, Sohee spoke.

'No, I'm going to choose something else.'

'Really?' Yeji looked surprised.

'Yeah. I'm thinking of the cooking club.' Sohee swallowed hard.

'You can cook?'

'Not really, but I want to try.'

Her lips were cracking. This was more nerve-wracking than acting in front of the whole school during the election speech. Her heart thumped so loudly that for a moment, she wondered if Yeji could also hear it.

Sohee was afraid to meet Yeji's eyes. She kept her gaze lowered, but luckily, the silence didn't drag out.

'Oh? All right, I'll join you.'

'Huh? You don't have to.'

Sohee felt a stab of guilt, as though she was taking Yeji away from the rest of their friends. Just as her anxiety threatened to peak, Yeji answered in a bright voice, 'But I've always wanted to learn cooking too!'

Their eyes met. Yeji was always honest with her feelings. Sohee had never seen her lie.

'That's great.'

Sohee nodded happily. The anxiety dissipated.

Creak—

Mun came in through the side door with his arms full. A mouth-watering aroma filled the air. Bo-reum scooted closer for a look.

'What did you buy?'

'Pizza. I ordered it online, but I had to go to the park to pick it up so that took a while. Want some?'

A riddle of words. Why did he have to go all the way to the

park to pick up pizza? Bo-reum was curious, but she decided not to pursue it. Even if she asked, it was obvious that she would only get another cryptic response.

Mun placed the pizza on the table, and next to it, a small glass bottle.

'Isn't this what you sold to the girl that day?'

'One got returned. Looks like she didn't need it anymore.'

Bo-reum picked up the bottle. Under the glow of the lights, the blue liquid shimmered. Thinking of the girl who had read her name tag as 'Bo-reum', she turned to Mun.

'Didn't you say that we have to be careful of those who can read our name tags differently? That we'll be dragged away?'

'Once the shop gets found out, they'll come for us. Didn't I mention this? This is an illegal business.'

Bo-reum's pupils dilated in fear.

Who will come for us?

Just as she was about to ask the question, she recalled what had happened at the library when the security alarms went off. How Mun turned from the custodian to a fugitive after interfering with the stories.

'Those who read my name tag as "Moon" are those who know what this place is. Engaging with them increases the risk of exposing what we do. If the library gets wind of what we're doing, maybe we'll have to move.'

'Then why do you still take their business?!'

Mun's answer was simple.

'Because they found us.'

Kung—

Mun put down a heavy iron ball by his feet. It was the payment he'd taken from the girl. Bo-reum stared at it. What use was he going to have for such a bulky thing?

'Actually, it's not so much about getting caught, but rather, it's not good for the customers. And it goes against my principles.'

Bo-reum slid down from her stool and took a closer look. It resembled the ball and chain attached to a prisoner's ankle. Etched on it were the words: EXPECTATIONS OF OTHERS.

'This shop is meant to be like a *mun* – a door – that people pass through. When customers come in, I serve them something and then it's time for them to go. But a moon – even if it sounds the same – is different. When people see the moon, they make a wish. But we are not here to grant wishes.'

Bo-reum nodded absentmindedly at his words. She glanced at the glass bottle on the table.

'It's amazing that you can whip up those magical concoctions.'

'You think so? To me, the ability to comfort a friend in need is much more special and magical.'

Chapter 6
The Second Farewell

It was a Friday evening. When the clock struck six, the bustling office quickly quietened as everyone left on the dot. For once, nobody would be working late.

'Have a good Chuseok break!'

On a desk calendar, the three-day national holidays were circled in red. Everyone was looking forward to the extra-long break which, including the weekend, would stretch for five days until the following Wednesday.

There were those who booked an overseas vacation; someone planned to spend the break binge-playing video games. Han Areum, who had just graduated from being the newbie in the office, was going back to her hometown.

I should hurry.

Areum took the airtight banchan container that she'd left in the office fridge and placed it into her travel bag. Because she planned to head to the train station straight from work, she had prepared the side dish beforehand and brought it with her this morning.

'I hope I'll make it in time.'

She grabbed her stuff, hurried to the subway station and pushed herself into the crowded train heading towards Seoul Station. Chuseok was the time of the mass exodus across the country, so the express train tickets had to be bought a month earlier. The tickets were quickly snapped up, so Areum had no choice but to book an earlier timing than she'd have preferred. If she didn't hurry, she might miss the train.

'Faster, faster,' she muttered under her breath.

At Seoul Station, rows of trains stood at the platform tracks, soon to depart to the different provinces in the country. Train timings and platform numbers flashed on the huge electronic screen. As she kept an ear out for the announcements blaring from the speakers, she weaved through the sea of people and took the escalator up to her platform, all the while anxiously checking the time. She spotted her train just right ahead. There were a few minutes left to board. However, she couldn't help but imagine that the train would depart right then, leaving her stranded on the platform.

'Ha— That was close.'

Luckily, none of that happened. Only when she settled down in her seat did the worry stop bubbling over. She triple-checked the train, carriage and seat number on her ticket before stretching her tense limbs and relaxing into the seat.

'*Welcome aboard the KTX bound for Busan. We'll do our best to make your journey as comfortable as possible.*'

Accompanied by a bright melody, the announcement filtered through the speakers. As the anxiety ebbed, a surge of eagerness filled her. It'd been a long time since she last went home.

How did I even end up living in Seoul . . . ?

Back in school, the thought of Seoul evoked more curiosity than any real longing to experience the bustle of the capital city. And she was curious only because it was her mum's hometown. Her mum grew up in Seoul and it was through her work that she travelled across the country and ended up meeting Areum's dad.

According to Mum, she didn't have the best impression of Dad at first, but he didn't give up and she eventually opened her heart to him. Whenever Mum talked about the courtship, Dad would only cough shyly. But when she said, 'I was lucky to have met the most affectionate person on earth,' the corners of his lips would lift visibly.

Areum yawned.

She stared at the scenery rolling past the window, but soon, everything looked the same and drowsiness set in. Whenever she was in a vehicle, instead of getting travel sick, she'd doze off easily. Same for trains.

She wondered sleepily if it was because of the comfort of knowing that she didn't have to do anything else and was just waiting to get to her destination. The seat wasn't as soft as a bed, but it was comfortable enough. Luckily, her compartment was relatively quiet. Areum closed her eyes and drifted off to sleep.

'. . . *because of a fault at the station, train services have stopped.*'

Awakened by the blaring announcement and the cacophony surrounding her, Areum opened her eyes blearily and looked around. At the sight of the frustrated faces, even though she was still half-asleep, immediately, she knew something was wrong.

'*A full refund will be given to affected passengers. Thank you for your kind understanding. Once again, we sincerely apologise for the inconvenience caused.*'

The announcement went on to advise affected passengers

to use alternative modes of transport. The sleepiness vanished in an instant. Other modes of transport? But it was Chuseok. Would there still be any seats left?

Where am I?

She quickly grabbed her travel bag from the rack above and got off the train. At the unfamiliar sights, her heart pounded.

The big clock on the train platform indicated that it was half past nine. Glancing at the station sign, Areum realised that she was at Ulsan Station, the neighbouring metropolitan city one stop away from Busan.

Please, please!

She quickly checked the other transport options on the app, but just as she had expected, everything was sold out. There was the option of taking a taxi, but it was going to be a lot more expensive. She massaged her throbbing temple.

'Ugh, not that I have a choice.'

Whining wasn't going to help the situation. She decided to call her parents first. Not wanting to make them more worried, she tried clearing her throat to relieve the tension in her voice as she waited for the call to connect.

'Areum-ah, are you on your way? I'm heading to Busan Station, so call me when you get there. I had an out-of-town business trip, and the meetings dragged on. I might be a little late, just finished work.'

'Don't worry. I'm running late, too.'

'Why? Was there a delay?'

'No. The train stopped. A track fault or something. Not a big deal . . .'

'Wait, what? Where are you? Are you still on the train? How's the situation?'

Areum thought she'd tried her best to sound calm, but on second thoughts, it was natural for her parents to be worried.

'Things are fine. I've alighted. I'm going to get a taxi from Ulsan Station.'

'You're at Ulsan? Okay. Since I'm on the way, I'll pick you up. Wait for me at the station.'

'Don't come all the way. I can just take a taxi.'

'Just wait for me. A taxi is going to cost a bomb! Anyway, it's cold, so don't stay in the station. Go find a restaurant or something.'

'I'm fine. It's not cold at all.'

'It's already autumn! Just listen to me. I'll take about an hour, so wait somewhere warm.'

'But—'

'No buts.'

Before she could say anything else, the line went dead.

'How is an hour's drive *on the way*?'

It was clearly a flimsy lie, but her anxious heart calmed down. *All right. Where should I go?*

Outside the station was a long line of taxis and buses. She looked around for a decent restaurant, but nothing caught her eye. For a while, she walked aimlessly and just as she was wondering if she should head back to the station, she spotted a dim light. Before she knew it, her footsteps had carried her to a small shop that gave off a mysterious aura compared to its surroundings.

IF YOUR LIFE WERE A BOOK

Looks decent.

The cosy shopfront matched her vibe. She turned the

handle, and the door creaked open as the chime tinkled. There were no customers at all. Was it because the shop was slightly off the main street?

'Welcome to the Moon Glow Bookshop.'

A waitress with bunny ears greeted her with a bright voice. Areum smiled, thinking about the folktale legend of the Moon Rabbit often told during Chuseok.

That's cute.

Areum followed the bobbing ears to her seat. Picking up the menu, she noticed the bottles of alcohol on the shelves. So, this was a bar. With its beautiful array of bottles and glassware, she'd initially thought this was a teahouse.

'Do you serve food?'

She took her eyes off the menu and looked up at the bartender. With striking blue hair, the man looked somewhat ethereal. She glanced at his name tag – *MUN*.

'If you order a drink, we'll offer a complimentary dish.'

'Whoa.'

This was the first time she'd heard of a place that offered free food with a drink.

They aren't going to serve me leftovers, right? Or are the drinks going to be expensive?

Areum glanced apprehensively at the menu. There wasn't a price list.

Surely a hole-in-the-wall shop won't . . .

Despite trying to reassure herself, Areum pointed at what looked like the cheapest thing on the menu.

'How much is this?'

'Oh. That's our Chuseok special drink.'

Smiling, the bartender quoted a price that was cheaper than what she had expected. In fact, it was about the price of a bottle of *soju* from a convenience store. She was only getting a glass instead of an entire bottle, but for wine or a cocktail, it was considered very affordable.

'I'll have this then.'

The bartender nodded.

The shaker looped gracefully from his right hand to his left, tossed casually into the air and spinning circles before he caught it easily. Areum's eyes were transfixed by his flashy sequence, and before she could blink, her drink was served. But that was not the end of the show.

Is this a magic trick?

Oiling a fry pan, he snapped his fingers several times and a fire whooshed beneath it. There wasn't a stove or anything. The man appeared to shake the pan in midair and suddenly the flames and smoke appeared.

The bunny-eared waitress passed him a bowl of beaten eggs, and like the cocktail, in no time a steaming egg roll was plated and served.

'Please enjoy.'

Her mouth watered at the rising aroma. She picked up a piece of egg roll and placed it in her mouth. Immediately, the soft fluffy egg melted, bringing out the flavours of the buttery cheese.

When had he added the cheese?

It was nothing like the egg rolls she had tried before, more like an omelette. But it was absolutely satisfying. As she chewed, her glance naturally landed on the cocktail. The shimmering blue reminded her of waves hitting the break-water, or perhaps the beautiful expanse of the autumn sky.

Looks delicious.

She swallowed the last bit of cheese in her mouth and lifted the glass to her lips. The cocktail didn't seem to give off any aroma. She took a mouthful, and a grunt escaped her as she swallowed.

'Ugh.'

The bitterness was so overpowering that she couldn't help but stick out her tongue. She covered her mouth belatedly, but the disgusting taste lingered. The bartender stood in front of her, and she didn't want to appear rude, but her brows creased involuntarily. To neutralise the yucky sensation on her palate, she quickly took another bite of the delicious egg roll.

How is this a complementary pairing?

The bar should just stick to being a restaurant. She lost all appetite for the drink. Instead, she picked up her phone and texted.

I'm at the small bar close to the station.

There was no reply. Probably still on the way, she thought.

It's so pretty though . . .

She could feel the heat of the alcohol rising in her. It must've been a stiff one. Gazing at it reminded her of the blue sea or the sky. A captivating cocktail, at least visually. Unfortunately, the taste didn't match up.

Or was it bitter because it was my first sip?

She tried another mouthful, but it was the same. This time, she'd prepared herself mentally, so before her expression changed, she immediately popped in another piece of egg roll.

'Huu—'

Every breath she drew in felt colder, and the breath she exhaled warmer. She could hold her drink quite well, but today, in just two mouthfuls, her cheeks were already flushed. There was still some left in the glass, but she had had enough.

Ugh.

Even when her expression scrunched up as the drink went down her throat, she looked at the shimmering liquid and found herself reaching for the glass again.

Something beside the heat from the alcohol was wriggling in her chest. Like the feeling of holding her breath, the pressure was building up and she felt an impulse to scream and let it all out.

Am I just too tired?

Suddenly, a wave of misery welled up in her. To make sure she could enjoy the holidays, she had to rush to clear her work. She must've gone beyond her threshold, burnt-out from the stress and the never-ending late nights.

But is that really the reason?

She was sure she hadn't felt this frustrated and sad even during that time she'd made a mistake and suffered the wrath of her boss.

Why am I feeling like this right now?

Just as the thoughts unspooled in her mind, the door chime tinkled.

'Areum-ah!'

'Mum?' Areum cried out in delight.

Turning around, she saw her mum smiling at her, and in that moment, all the frustrations and heaviness in her chest melted away.

'Oof. The smell of alcohol. You can't even hold your drink, what are you doing at a bar? Have you eaten? What's that – egg rolls? Is that enough? You need rice.'

Her mum began her incessant nagging as she took the seat

next to her. Areum resisted the urge to throw herself into her mum's arms and sob. Instead, she jutted out her lip, her tone brusque.

'I'm not a child! And please, I *can* hold my drink.'

'Ha. You should see your face – all red. Do you still have your wits about you now?' Tut-tutting, her mum shook her head.

'Mum, why did you have to say that?' Areum protested.

'*Aigoo*, that temper of yours. Baring your claws at me, *tsk*,' said her mum, chuckling.

Areum's pout lifted to a smile, and in that moment, a surge of feelings broke through the dam and tears were free-falling down her cheeks.

'Ah . . .'

Areum was flustered. Why did she burst into tears when it wasn't something to cry about? Her mum pulled out several tissues and dabbed her cheeks.

'What's wrong? Have things been tough?'

Her mum's embrace, her warm hand patting her back, filled Areum with comfort. Wedged in her mum's arms, the space was tighter than being in a car or train, but the snugness that filled her was incomparable. When her heaving tapered to a quiet sob, her mum chuckled.

'That said, you're really unlucky. Of all the trains, yours had to stop midway.'

'At least it reached Ulsan,' Areum retorted, her voice hoarse.

Her mum continued teasing her despite her attempts to soothe her just a moment ago.

'All grown-up but your tears have yet to dry! Crying like a baby in your mum's arms. If you still want to cry, at least get a boyfriend to wipe your tears for you. It'd be nice if you could meet a guy like your dad and bring him home to meet us.'

'Mum! I'm still young.'

'Who's asking you to get married? I'm telling you to date if you meet someone decent. Then I don't have to worry for you. I've done enough of that!'

'Whatever. Mum, you're mean,' Areum protested, but she held on tight to her mum's arm.

'How much longer are you going to behave like a child? I can't stay by your side for ever. When I die, are you going to come crying to me at my grave?'

'Mum! Don't talk about dying!'

It'd always been like this. Her mum always had the power to make her upset with her words.

'Let's see if you'll still come to me when you have a boyfriend. You'll probably stick to him and forget all about me.'

'I'm bringing you on our dates.'

'Ha! What an affectionate child! *Tsk*. And what are the three of us supposed to do? Play Go-Stop cards?'

Areum was annoyed. But she knew that she'd always be on the losing end in an argument with her mum, so she pursed her lips tight. The only thing she could do to rebel was to wriggle out of her mum's embrace and pout.

'Whatever. I want to go home.'

'Oh yeah, it's about time.'

Areum touched her glass – there was still some left. She didn't want to finish her drink, but her mum was watching, and she didn't want to give her more reason to tease her about not being able to hold her drink. Suddenly, Areum remembered the travel bag at her feet.

'Oh right. I made something.'

'You cooked? You can cook?'

'Hmph. Mum, stop doubting my abilities. I made japchae. We can put it on the offering table when we perform the charye memorial service.'

Areum unzipped the bag and took out the airtight container wrapped in layers of clothes. It was filled to the brim with the sweet potato starch noodles stir-fry.

'You should've made the jeon pancake that your dad loves.'

'But Mum, you love these noodles, don't you!'

'Huh?'

'After every memorial service, you'd always eat the japchae. That's why I made this . . .'

Why though? Areum suddenly asked herself. Of all dishes, why japchae? It's for the memorial service for their ancestors, so why did she only make the food Mum likes? Her mum was obviously the better cook, so why did she bother? And she could've just bought it from a nearby market, why did she go to the trouble of bringing it in an airtight container to the office?

As the thoughts unspooled in her mind, the pressure in her chest was building up again. A vague memory that hung at the back of her mind sharpened. Her breathing hitched.

'Mum?' Areum turned around.

Her mum's hair was sleek, and her skin smooth. Like back in the past. Wait. Why did she think that? As if it was impossible in the present.

'Why did you hide it from me?'

The smile on her mum's face vanished.

Don't say it. Don't say it. Don't!

Alarm bells rang in Areum's head, and despite a voice warning her to keep quiet, her lips moved of their own accord.

'If you're sick, you should've told me. Why did you hide it from me? Do you know how terrible it feels, the betrayal? Why! Why didn't you tell me . . .?'

Because she'd been living in Seoul even before getting a job, she had been away from home for a long time.

In this time, what had she been so busy with? Why was it that she could find time to do small favours for her boss, listen patiently to the clients cracking lame jokes . . . yet she didn't have a moment to spare for her mum?

Cancer – the disease that scraped her mum empty from the inside. Her mum had refused to tell her anything, saying that it'd cause her unnecessary worries. Why make things worse for her daughter who should be focused on finding a job, why disturb her when she was struggling to adapt to working life . . .?

It was only much later that Areum learned about her mum's sickness. Mum, who had lost so much weight by then, looked very different from how she remembered. Areum was now working. She could now afford to buy her mum delicious food, take her to nice places; she could finally take care of her. But Mum didn't wait for her.

She begged for forgiveness. Begged for a second chance from God. Nothing else mattered. She only wanted her mum to be healthy. She begged hard. *Not a malignant tumour. Not metastasis.* However, it was not to be. Last winter, Mum had left her for ever.

'Mum, you were having a hard time, right?'

Splash. The tears were blurring her vision. She forced herself to focus; she didn't want to lose her mum again.

'Mum, you must've been in so much pain . . .'

Her mum reached out a hand and brushed aside Areum's fringe.

'I'm sorry. I didn't want you to see me sick. And congrats, my dear daughter. For getting into the company that you were aiming for. I'm sorry I couldn't celebrate with you.'

'What's the point of saying this now?'

Even as Areum was mired in anguish and anger, her mum simply looked at her.

'I still can't believe that you're no longer by my side. When I come back home, it feels like you're just a call away. I miss you so much . . .'

Areum leaned forward and hugged her mum tight, her face awash with tears.

'Can't you not go? Can you stay by my side?'

A soft hand stroked her hair gently, and her mum's kindly voice rang in her ears.

'Do you remember that time, back in middle school, or was it high school? You were so upset that your bedroom door didn't have a lock, and you yelled at me?'

Areum remembered. She was in her rebellious teens. That day, she was annoyed when her mum came into her room. She screamed that she was a grown-up, that it was an invasion of her privacy. She was so upset that her parents had to change her door handle so that she could lock her door if she wanted.

'Didn't you insist that you needed privacy? I need mine now, too. Do you think I'm spending all my time looking at you? No way. And now you're a grown-up too, I don't have to keep watching over you.'

Areum tried to hold her mum tight, but somehow it felt like her mum was getting lighter and lighter, just as she had grown emaciated because of her illness.

'Areum-ah, just think of me occasionally. Don't keep me on your mind all the time; I need my own space too.'

Her mum tried to make light of things, but Areum could hear the tremble in her voice. She choked up; it was time to say goodbye.

'Mum, there are so many things I haven't done for you.'

'Then treat your dad well.'

Mum's voice was fading. Her touch dissipated. On the table, the glass with the bitter liquor was empty. But her mum's warmth lingered, wrapping itself around Areum's exhausted body.

'Areum-ah! Didn't I tell you to wait inside a restaurant? Why are you out here?'

'Dad?'

Areum opened her eyes only to find herself squatting by the roadside. She looked around, but the enigmatic shop was nowhere in sight. Only a pair of worried eyes were looking down on her. Just like how he had sounded over the phone at the station, her dad's voice now was laced with worry.

'You've been drinking?'

'Only a little.'

'Let's go. You're going to catch a cold like this.'

She got into the car. Summer had passed and the wind was chilly, but her body felt warm, as though someone was hugging her.

'Sorry I'm late. The traffic was bad.'

'Do you still go on business trips often?'

'Hmm? Yeah.'

Areum glanced at her dad's side profile. Since when had he grown so wrinkled?

'It must be tough, right? To be away so often.'

'It's fine. If I stay at home alone too much, I get bored.'

Flicking a glance at the travel bag on the backseat, Areum slowly spoke. 'Dad . . . Did Mum like japchae?'

After her mum's passing, Areum rarely spoke about her with her dad. For a moment, he was flustered. Then a gentle smile appeared on his lips.

'I think she hated it. You too, right? Both of you share the same tastebuds. Your grandpa was the one who loved the noodles.'

Areum always saw her mum eating the japchae after the memorial rites. So she had thought that her mum liked it. Come to think of it, it must be because Areum refused to have any.

She swallowed the painful lump in her throat and with difficulty, croaked out, 'I met Mum.'

'Huh?'

'After I had a few drinks, I dozed off and dreamt of her. But it feels like she really came to see me.'

Her dad glanced at her uncertainly. For a while, he kept quiet. Then he gave a light nod.

'Was she beautiful?'

'Yeah, very. She didn't look ill at all.'

Dad's eyes reddened. He sniffed once.

'That's great,' he said calmly.

'Yeah.'

The car cruised down the road back home.

'You can let a customer meet a person who has passed away?'

Sniffling, Bo-reum turned to Mun. Her eyes were bloodshot.

'Because today is Chuseok. The day the gates of the moon

open. I didn't make them meet, I simply allowed them to see the person who has crossed the boundary wanting to come and meet them.'

'I've guarded the moon for a long time, yet you know more than I do.'

'I didn't know either. But someone taught me.'

'Who?'

Mun flicked a glance at her before turning away to arrange the glasses neatly.

'Someone.'

She'd expected a riddle-like answer, but this time he refused to say more, as though it was a secret. She thought it strange, but his expression was a little stiff, so she decided not to probe. Instead, she asked another question.

'Have you ever experienced the pain of parting?'

'Yes.'

'You did?'

That was surprising. It felt as though he was only a door's span away from anyone and anywhere. If there was someone he missed, he could just go to meet them right away.

'Who was it? Were you sad? Did you cry?'

'Of course. At the time, eating the most scrumptious delicacies felt like chewing mud, a walk in the most picturesque scenery was like passing through dead air,' Mun said as he washed the dishes.

It was hard to tell if he was being serious or joking.

'Tasty delicacies and beautiful scenery . . . Sounds like a break-up trip?'

'I suppose it's a trip of sorts. But instead of wanting to go somewhere, I wanted to escape reality.'

Without that playful glint in his eyes, he looked a little sad.

'The memories are too ingrained in the everyday moments. Thinking about it every so often hurts.'

'Hmm.'

The sorrow in his voice spilled over to her. Feeling like her reddened eyes were going to tear up again, she twitched her ears in a pretence of indifference.

'Do you still miss the person?'

He didn't avert his gaze. And as usual, he smiled.

'No, I'm good now.'

Chapter 7

The Young Man Who Became an Old Man

Huff, puff.

Bo-reum kicked the ground hard as she ran. Beads of sweat on her forehead flew in the wind, and her lungs stung as she gasped for breath. Yet, no matter how hard she ran, she couldn't shake them off.

'Stop. I am commanding you to stop, Bo-reum. You're surrounded. Stop immediately.'

Lights flashing as rapidly as her pounding heart were closing in on her. She was a strong rabbit. Strong enough to be a guardian of the universe. All she needed was to focus and her smooth, thin legs could become muscular in a second.

But why is it not working?

For some reason, her body refused to listen to her commands. Almost as if someone had bound her legs to a weight, preventing them from transforming.

That wasn't the worst. No matter how fast she ran, the surroundings remained unchanged. It was like running on a treadmill.

Huff, puff.

While Bo-reum remained stuck on the same spot, the red and blue flashing lights were closing in on her. The robots with sirens on their heads glared at her with ferocious eyes. Panic seized her.

'Nooooo!'

Her arm was held in a tight grip by cold steel fingers. She screamed, but the robots ignored her. The next second, her world turned black; she was being tossed somewhere.

Bloop, bloop—

Bo-reum felt the odd sensation of being thrown into an empty, dark night sky. She lost her sense of direction; everything was spinning. All she could do was to flail her limbs helplessly.

'Ah!'

She felt a firm grip on her shoulder, holding her in place. Suddenly, her surroundings brightened, as if someone had yanked off a black cloth. Bo-reum realised that she was sitting on a hard chair.

Where am I?

A single bare bulb glowed. The narrow shaft of light illuminated a square table and a recording device on it.

'Speak only the truth.'

'Lying will only add to your charges!'

Across the table were two detectives who looked like giant lightbulbs themselves. Steel arms poked out from their bodies, with the eyes, nose and lips drawn on with markers. When they spoke, they glowed a bright red and blue respectively.

They look like Christmas baubles.

At that thought, the tension in her shoulders slipped away. Noticing the slight lift of her lips, Red Lightbulb snarled.

'DO WE LOOK LIKE WE'RE JOKING?'

Crack—!

Red Lightbulb smashed his head on the table and with a

sharp crash, the glass shards flew in all directions. When he looked up again, Bo-reum screamed inwardly.

Red Lightbulb leaned forward with its sharp, jagged edges frighteningly close. Cold sweat trailed down her spine. He looked ready to stab her if she dared to lie.

'You've broken space laws. You're aware of that, right?' Blue Lightbulb spoke in a steely voice. It seemed like he had no intention of stopping his partner's intimidating antics.

What are you talking about?! Bo-reum wanted to retort, but at the sight of the photo on the table, she clamped her mouth shut.

'This is a hardened criminal who regularly steals books from Library 527. A clear transgression of Article 3 Item 29 under the intergalactic space laws.'

Blue Lightbulb jabbed hard with his metallic finger. The person in the photo was none other than her boss – Mun.

'We have much reason to suspect that you're his accomplice.'

Blue Lightbulb glared at her as he flipped through a thick file.

'I . . .'

Blue Lightbulb slammed the file on the table with a loud thud.

'Look! We have CCTV images from Library 527! Do you not admit your wrongdoing!'

It was an image from the day they'd gone shopping for ingredients. Next to Mun was Bo-reum – her long bunny ears clearly visible.

'Th-this . . .'

'Enough excuses! If you confess to your crimes, we'll take that into consideration during the trial.'

'Speak the truth!'

Their voices rang threateningly. The red and blue lights pierced through her composure.

'I-I . . .'

'How long do you think you can keep up with your lies?'

'Death! Death penalty!'

Why is this happening to me?!

Squinting in the harsh light, she made out a silhouette in the corner. Mun was leaning against the wall, looking supremely unconcerned.

'Manager Mun!' she yelled desperately. His eyes flicked up to hers with an amused smile playing on his lips. Meanwhile, the lightbulbs thundered.

'We'll not fall for your lies! You've been caught!'

'Admit it! Tell the truth! Now!'

Their voices were getting louder, as if someone was turning up the volume. Just then, Mun spoke.

'Having a nightmare?'

The moment his lips moved, the loud roaring in her ears quietened at once. The lightbulbs were still staring menacingly at her, but the only voice in her ears was Mun's.

A nightmare?

Was it as Mun said? Just a dream?

'CONFESS!'

Once Mun stopped talking, the voices returned as if the volume was dialled up once more on the remote control. Their sharp voices pierced her ears uncomfortably.

'How do I wake up from this dream?' she shouted, desperate to leave the place.

'Stick out your tongue and make a funny face.'

Huh. However, she'd long given up on expecting something

logical from Mun, so she stuck out her tongue as far as she could and made a face.

Oh God. How long do I have to stay in this position?

She flicked her gaze at Mun, who was holding his belly and laughing his head off. Wiping away his tears, he spoke.

'Okay, I lied.'

'What?!'

Her anger boiled over as she flushed a deep red. At the same time, her arm muscles bulged rapidly. She shoved the lightbulbs out of the way with ease.

'Good job,' said Mun.

Even before Bo-reum realised what had just happened, Mun reached for the door handle behind him.

'Wait for me!'

Mun opened the door and stepped through. Angry, she quickly followed him.

'Ah!'

The ground ended abruptly where the door frame was. Bo-reum lurched forward. Flailing her limbs, she plunged into the darkness.

Thud—!

Bo-reum jerked up and realised she'd been sleeping face down on the table. She cast her bleary eyes around. Her arms were still rock hard. She quickly swiped away the streak of saliva dribbling from the corner of her mouth and relaxed her muscles.

Oh, it was a dream.

She checked her arms, now back to normal, and surveyed her surroundings. Luckily, no one was watching her.

Clank, clank—

Hearing sounds from the kitchen, Bo-reum went to check it out. Mun, with his back to her, was busy cooking. Thankfully, he didn't seem to have noticed her dozing off.

'What are you making?'

'Pumpkin soup.'

Mun's kitchen was quite unlike what you'd expect in a hole-in-the-wall shop. In contrast to the tiny shopfront, the kitchen was as big as what you'd find in a full-scale restaurant, and as well-equipped.

Bo-reum turned to the source of the heat. Placed neatly in a row were the stolen books. On top of each book was a pot, its contents changing colour according to the light from the book. Although, Bo-reum was clueless about the mechanics of this process.

'That's not on the menu.'

'I just wanted to try making it.'

Bo-reum tilted her head a fraction and scooted closer. On the table lay a few left-over wedges of pumpkin. By the looks of it, it was a regular pumpkin. And below the pot from which the delicious aroma wafted was not a book, but a regular stove.

'You like pumpkin soup?' Bo-reum edged a little closer to Mun and took a long, contented sniff.

'Not really. This is the first time I'm making it from scratch.'

Bo-reum looked up in surprise. Because he could whip up the most mysterious concoctions, she never thought that there could be any dishes he had never tried making.

Mun mumbled to himself, 'Why did I think of making this? I'm not hungry; it's not even my favourite soup.'

'Well, you've always been eccentric. But it smells delicious. For a first try, this smells really good.'

Mun ladled out the soup, but he was still looking pensive, as if he couldn't understand his own actions. However, seeing Bo-reum's star-filled eyes following his every action, the answer came to him. He relaxed.

'I'm guessing this is your favourite?'

'Hm? Yeah, I do like it.'

Even as she pretended to be indifferent, deep down, she was anxious that Mun wouldn't offer her a bowl. It was one of her favourite dishes; one that she would be happy having for all three of her daily meals.

'I guess I made it for you.'

Chuckling, he carried the bowl to the dining area, trailed by an eager Bo-reum. He sat down at a two-person table. But there was only one bowl and one spoon on the table.

'Try it. It should be quite delicious.'

Mun gestured to the seat opposite him. Bo-reum sat down. The bowl of soup was set right in front of her.

'Aren't you going to have some?'

'It's okay. I made it for you.'

'What? Really? But why?'

'I'm still figuring that out.'

Instead of saying something like *I thought you might be hungry* or *I'm just experimenting with a new dish*, he said he was still figuring it out. She eyed him beadily.

'Is it about *that* again?'

'About what?'

Knitting her brows, she deliberately cleared her throat and lowered her voice. '"*Here is where chance becomes destiny. There must be a reason why I made this soup,*" Am I right?'

Mun nodded. Bo-reum just wanted to tease him. To see him so agreeable was a little disconcerting.

'Um. If this is destiny, I'd welcome it with open arms,' she joked.

Bo-reum picked up the spoon and turned her focus back to the soup. She couldn't resist the mouthwateringly delicious aroma wafting up to her nostrils.

'If chance is destiny, then what is destiny?'

She wasn't that curious. She simply wanted to divert his attention so that she could slurp the soup without having to talk. And it looked like she had succeeded. For a while, Mun was locked in his thoughts. When he finally answered, all she had to do was to listen and murmur an appropriate response while enjoying her soup.

'It's just like how I opened a shop here, serve stories to the customers, listen to their stories, the same way someone else will be reading our stories in the future . . . everything is destined. You coming to work here was destiny too.'

Bo-reum nodded solemnly. But she was only half-listening. Her attention was on the rich flavours that glided across her tongue, the aroma swirling in her nostrils. How was this a first attempt? Mun was a master of soup dishes.

'And . . .'

'Hmm?'

Bo-reum glanced up. She nodded vigorously, as if to prove that she was listening.

'I must be destined to cook for an employee who takes naps during work hours.'

She choked.

Mun watched her cough and splutter as he poured her a glass of water. She quickly gulped it down.

'Because it's getting cold,' she said defensively between coughs.

'Since when do rabbits hibernate?'

Bo-reum wondered if she should insist that her species did, but in the end, she kept quiet. No matter how harsh winter was on earth, it'd never get as cold as the moon.

'You saw me?'

Mun gestured at the mirror on the wall, indicating that she take a look herself. Despite the mirror being some distance away, she could see the distinct red mark on her forehead, the kind one gets when sleeping with their forehead on the table.

'Oh damn. I've been going around advertising that I'm the culprit!' she exclaimed, rubbing her forehead ruefully.

Her mood soured. The word 'culprit' reminded her of her dream. Mun didn't miss the frown that flashed across her face.

'Had a bad dream?'

Bo-reum hesitated. Should she talk about it? As though making up her mind, she let out a long sigh.

'It was an odd dream. Someone was chasing me, and no matter how hard I tried to escape, I kept going in circles. And I got caught in the end.'

Thinking about the menacing lightbulbs, she shivered. Especially Red Lightbulb. The image of the glass shattering in all directions was etched on her mind.

'Why were you being chased?'

'They discovered the shop. Didn't you tell me that this is an illegal operation, and we might get caught anytime? I guessed it weighed on me.'

Saying it aloud helped her to better understand her anxiety. Indeed, Mun's words had been bugging her – that they'd better be careful when dealing with customers who called them Moon and Bo-reum because they came in with the knowledge that this wasn't a normal bar. And how it'd increase the chances of the shop, and them, being exposed.

The dream might've been a reflection of her anxiety, but there was a very real possibility of getting caught. In fact, the thick file that Blue Lightbulb slammed on the table was identical to the actual book on space laws.

'Do you know anything about the space laws?'

'A little.'

'Then do you know what Article 3 Item 29 is about?'

A legal text was also a book, and Mun was like a walking encyclopaedia of books. He fell into thought before exclaiming as though he'd just remembered the spelling of a complicated word from a long vocabulary list.

'It's something to do with theft.'

Bo-reum drew a sharp breath. Was that really a dream? And if so, a clairvoyant one?

She chose her next words carefully. 'Is there a species in the universe that look like lightbulbs? Like the universe's police, or . . .'

She watched Mun anxiously. Mun stared back and a shiver ran down her spine.

'Oh my God . . .' She blanched.

Mun burst out into laughter. The same irritating laughter she remembered in her dream.

'What are you laughing at?'

'The breadth of your imagination. You met the universe's police? And they look like *lightbulbs*?'

Her brows furrowed. 'Don't laugh . . . Then when you were saying that Article 3 Item 29 is about theft . . .'

'That bit is real,' Mun said, stifling his laughter.

It was a mixed bag of feelings. On one hand, she wanted to

dismiss it as a ridiculous dream, but it was hard to ignore it completely when some things were eerily real.

'Even if it was just my nightmare, can we please stop accepting customers who know who we are? It's too dangerous.'

'You sure? This means you might not get a bonus.'

'Well, it beats getting caught. And didn't you say that it also goes against your principles?'

This place is a door to pass through, not a place to grant wishes.

Bo-reum's mood dampened as she recalled what he'd said. It was like stamping out her own vague hope that in this magical place, her wish could come true.

'Okay,' Mun replied.

Bo-reum gave a start. She'd never imagined that he'd agree so easily.

'What?'

'Then I have to shut down the website too. And hide our location on the street, so that people can't find us so easily.'

'W-wait. Isn't this too sudden? And I'm just a staff member, you don't . . .'

Mun didn't sound like he was joking. The thought that she was the one barring the customers from the shop made her uneasy.

'But isn't this the place where chance turns into destiny? And even those who came knowing what this place sells also found their way here by chance.'

She looked at Mun, who simply shrugged.

'That's what chances are, isn't it? Out of the many possible permutations, things just happen in a particular way. That you came to work here, and even you offering a suggestion right now is one of the many possibilities of all the things that could happen.'

'But . . .'

'Instead of overthinking it, let's just give it a try. In any case, what will happen will happen.'

What will happen will happen.

Somehow, those words gave her comfort. And she was also grateful that Mun was willing to listen to her.

A warm energy pooled in her chest, the same feeling as enjoying a hearty bowl of soup. She nodded happily.

Tinkle—

A gust of wind blew in as the door opened. An old man in a heavy coat stepped inside.

'It's getting chilly.'

He dusted off his trousers, and tiny flakes as white as his hair fell to the ground. It must be snowing heavily outside. Bo-reum quickly grabbed a menu and went to greet him.

'Like you said, this place hasn't changed at all,' said the old man as he glanced at Bo-reum, his creased eyes crinkling in a smile.

Bo-reum raised an eyebrow but kept quiet.

He looked around the shop, as though reliving an old memory. Slowly, he moved to the counter seat opposite the bartender. Sensing that this was no usual customer, Bo-reum quickly pointed at her name tag.

'If you don't mind, can you read out what is written on my tag?'

The old man glanced at it before returning his gaze to her. He stuck out a hand.

'Please to meet you, Bo-reum-ssi.'

'Ah, same here.'

Flustered by his formal ways, she quickly shook his hand.

It was only a moment later that she realised that he had called her Bo-reum.

Calm down, relax.

Red sirens were flashing in her head. Was this man going to apprehend them for operating an illegal business? Cold sweat trickled down her spine.

'I believe this isn't your first visit, am I right?'

Mun smiled at him. Only then did Bo-reum let out the breath she'd been holding. The old man laughed heartily and nodded.

'No, I don't think it is. If my memory serves me right.'

It'd been a long time since the elderly man had laughed so easily, as if he was a young man again. The last time he came to the shop was about fifty years ago. Memories from those years were as fragile as dried leaves, but the magician, if he could call him that, remained vividly imprinted on his mind.

'I heard you always look up at the moon. Do you still do that these days?' Mun asked.

'Of course. Each time I think of this place, and that's almost every day . . .'

The old man nodded wistfully, but the next moment, perhaps having recalled something, sadness clouded his eyes.

'Actually, that's not true. I haven't been doing that for the past year. Because it feels like making a futile wish.'

Mun nodded, as if he could also empathise with him. He cleared away the menu and placed a champagne flute in front of the man. The clear glass held a sparkling red drink, bubbles rising to the surface.

'Didn't we agree not to sell to customers who know about this place?' Bo-reum hissed and elbowed Mun in his side.

However, it didn't seem like he was going to take away the glass from the customer. She glared at him, but he shrugged.

'This is an exception; we have to close the loop.'

'To close the loop? What're you on about? What are you serving him?'

'A drink that'll allow him to meet his younger self from fifty years ago. Fifty years ago, not on this exact day though, he had a drink and met with his older self from fifty years in the future.'

Alarm bells rang in her head. Even though she didn't know much about the space–time continuum, it was common knowledge that laws of space–time were the most fastidious, never to be interfered with due to the possibility of irreversible consequences.

'Why would you serve something so risky?'

The comfort she'd felt a moment ago from his words vanished in an instant. *Things that will happen will happen* no longer had a positive spin to her ears. There was no way things could end well. She could already see herself being held responsible in court and having her sentence meted out.

'I just happened to have all the right ingredients, and as soon as I had finished preparing the drink, the customer walked in. It was all impeccable timing. And, well, it was fifty years ago. I had no fear. It was all *shoot first, ask questions later.*'

For something that had potentially disastrous repercussions, Mun was being completely blasé, recounting it as though it was some childhood mischief. Bo-reum privately thought that it was a miracle the shop had managed to last till today.

Just as she was thinking of a good retort, the old man stared at the champagne flute and spoke, his eyes glistening with the memories of days long passed.

'This brings back old memories.'

'I hope you'll have a good time.'

For a while, the old man simply stared at the glass, as if captivated by the bubbles. He shifted his shoulders several times but always stopped short of reaching for the drink.

Finally, his fingers, which hovered over the glass, touched it with a clear tinkle that broke the silence.

'It's been a long time since I had a drink. My wife used to fret about my health. Her nagging served as a very effective deterrent.'

Raising the flute to his lips, the sweet aroma enveloped his senses. As the drink glided past his tongue and down his throat, memories of his youth flashed across his mind. Like the previous time many years ago, he knocked it back in one.

'Huu—'

The heat that rose at the back of his throat escaped as he exhaled. Was he getting on in age? Or was the drink too strong? Already, he had to will himself to maintain a clear mind.

Like an attack of vertigo, the world spun for a moment, and suddenly, the noises from his surroundings faded into silence. He looked up. Where there had been a plain wall, a door appeared. A dark blue door. The man got up and slowly walked towards it.

'How warm,' he muttered as he stepped through the door. The snugness seemed at odds with the wintry weather outside.

In the room were two comfortable armchairs that stood on either side of a round table. As he sat down, the old man exhaled a warm breath and glanced at a yellow door at the opposite end of the room. He didn't have to wait long.

'Ugh, so cold.'

The door opened, and a young man walked in. He was wearing a summer suit and at the sudden draught from entering the cold room, he hunched forward.

'You . . .'

In contrast to the young man's shock, the old man looked up calmly.

'Come, sit down.'

The young man's eyes widened and darted around nervously. Even as he pulled back the chair, he didn't take his eyes off the old man. Noticing his tense demeanour, like a porcupine wary of a stranger, the old man gave a wry smile.

'Did you come from the future . . .?' the young man asked.

'Yes, I'm your future.'

The young man swallowed hard. He stared into the old man's eyes, the exact colour of his own, and lifted a hand carefully to his face as if trying to find the wrinkles that would appear in years to come.

There was only a table between the two chairs. But as they held each other's gaze, it felt as though they were looking into a mirror.

'I've aged so much.'

They appeared so alike. Yet, if one looked carefully, there were many differences – the colour of the hair, the number of wrinkles, the look in their eyes. And even the set of their mouths. So similar, yet different.

'Is there anything you're curious about?' the old man asked.

Just like how a constant drip of water could dig a deep hole, and the winds could erode the sturdiest rock, the intervening years between them had dulled many of his memories.

He couldn't quite remember what they'd spoken about the last time they had met. What lingered in his mind was a vague recollection of the mood back then, and how his older self had asked him what he was curious about.

Is this for real?

Meanwhile, the young man stared at the elderly man opposite him. Despite their uncanny resemblance, it was hard to believe this was real.

Am I in a dream?

After getting rejected by yet another theatre company that he had auditioned with, he'd been feeling dispirited the entire day. All he wanted to do was drown his sorrows. Touching the few crumpled notes in his pocket, he had stepped inside a dingy-looking bar, perhaps attracted by how the small shop, like him, must struggle to stay afloat.

'Thank you for being my first customer. Please enjoy this on the house.'

The staff had greeted him in delight and immediately served him a drink. He was suspicious that the waitress might have some tricks up her sleeve, but her bright smile assuaged his wariness.

The sight of her long bunny ears had initially alarmed him, but she was very good at putting people at ease and he found himself opening up about his anxieties.

'I'm really worried about my future. I don't know what's going to happen,' he blurted out, feeling a little light-headed from the very first sip.

'Then, how about you meet your future and find out for yourself?'

The young man burst into laughter. However, the woman calmly put a glass down in front of him and told him that this next drink would allow him to meet his future self.

'That would be cool.'

It wasn't that he believed her. All he wanted was to forget his reality, even if just for a moment. So he nodded and knocked back the drink.

Just as the woman had promised, here he was, sitting face to face with his older self.

'May I know which year in the future you've come from?'

'About fifty years from your time.'

Fifty years. That was almost twice his current age. With flushed cheeks, he moved his lips several times as if to say something, but he had no idea where to begin.

'Will I go into acting? No, wait. Will I be famous? Or will I end up doing something else? If so, what is it? How do I age? Will I fall sick?'

The words tumbled out of him as he asked all the questions he could think of.

'Is there something I should avoid? I mean, what should I be careful of? Or can you tell me the winning lottery numbers?'

The old man simply gazed at him. Like a drop of water in boiling oil, he watched the young man's sudden enthusiasm explode in all directions. He felt an unexpected and deep longing for his youth and, he had to admit, a touch of envy.

Ah, so that was how I looked.

To the old man, his younger face looked a little awkward. To practise acting, he'd spent hours in front of the mirror making different expressions, but outside of acting, he had no interest in how he expressed himself. The old man finally realised why his younger self kept getting rejected from the theatre troupes.

'Do *you* ever memorise lottery numbers? Down to the exact order and the date?'

The young man froze. Indeed, nobody would think to remember past lottery numbers. He didn't, so it would be preposterous to expect the old man to. He tried to hide his disappointment.

'Scoring something nice without putting in the hard work feels great, of course. But there's also nothing emptier and more meaningless than that. Especially when it's something important to you.'

The old man continued to answer the other questions.

'Whatever you end up doing, at my age, you're going to be heading towards retirement. Sickness? Who doesn't have some aches and pains here and there at my age? What shouldn't you do? If the doctor tells you not to do something, like drinking and smoking, listen to them. Best if you can exercise regularly.'

He wasn't saying anything new. It was as if he was reciting textbook answers. The way his eyes roved slowly made it seem as though he was deliberately withholding answers, and it annoyed the young man. He mulled over what else to ask so that the old man couldn't give him vague answers like these.

The old man broke the silence, as though he'd read his mind. 'Sorry, but I don't plan on telling you much.'

'Why?'

'Because I hope that your future doesn't change.'

Because I'll be successful?

The young man was confused. Even if life was smooth sailing, how could it be that there was nothing at all that the older man would want to change?

'Does that mean you don't have any regrets?'

The old man, who was wearing a faint smile, slowly shook his head.

'How's that possible? From tiny mistakes to terrible choices, I can think of so many. After all, it's impossible for life to always go according to our plans.'

'If so, then why . . .'

The old man fell silent and twisted the ring on his left hand. He needed a moment to remember his resolve back when he was young. At his age, most memories had faded, but there was something that remained etched in his heart.

'Why did you quit the textile factory?'

The young man had been a manager at a big textile factory. He was hardworking, and well-liked. The pay wasn't half bad. When he quit, everyone tried to dissuade him: *'Quitting a stable job to join an acting troupe? Are you out of your mind?'*

But despite the less than enthusiastic response from everyone around him, he didn't waver in his decision.

'I wanted to challenge myself.'

That's just the drunken courage of youth, someone told him. He couldn't disagree completely, but the passion in him burned too brightly to be extinguished.

'But surely you'd have known that it wouldn't be an easy path?' the old man asked.

Indeed, one after another came the rejections. At first, he could still press on. In fact, he was spurred on to work even harder. But the never-ending string of failures cut deep; he felt worthless. He became anxious, and his resolve wavered.

'Of course I have.'

The young man tried to recall the days when his passion had burned bright. Compared to the old man, that wasn't such a long time ago, so it wasn't hard to remember. And that passion still resided in him.

'Everyone said I was going to fail. And I also imagined that things wouldn't work out the way I hoped they would.'

'Then why did you still do something so reckless? Aren't you scared?'

Is this really the right choice? In fact, the person questioning him the most was none other than himself. Over and over again, he asked himself. Again and again, he answered.

'Even if I'd known that I would fail, I'd still have made the same choice. Even if it's failure, I want to experience it for myself. Of course I was scared. But I didn't want to give up before I even got started.'

The old man looked at his younger self. All he did was to help him rediscover the seed of passion in him that he'd forgotten, but it was like lighting a fire with dry firewood – his eyes shone bright.

'To face the unknown is scary. However, if you close your eyes because you're scared, the fear will overshadow you. I didn't want that. I chose to challenge myself. I wanted to face the unknown head on – to discover how far I can go, what I'm capable of.'

His breath felt hot, like the heat of alcohol. The old man, who'd been watching him silently, spoke. 'I respect the younger me. Or I should say, I have deep admiration for you.

Even when faced with darkness ahead, you walk on confidently, on your own terms.'

He carefully removed his ring.

'I am who you make me to be. If you chase money, I'll be rich; if you seek power, I'll have authority. What you choose to keep close and pursue is your choice. Even if you don't hear the answer from me, you'll be able to find it in your heart.'

With a soft thud, he put down the ring on the table and slid it towards the younger man.

'It's okay to take breaks in life. But sadly, you can't undo the past. Every choice comes with regrets. Nevertheless, I hope that you'll choose what fits you the best.'

His gnarled hand lingered on the ring, as if reluctant to part with it. He let out a long sigh, as if the time had come to finish what he needed to do. Slowly, he pulled away.

'We should go. Can you give this ring to the shop owner and tell her it's for the drinks?'

The old man got up and smoothed the creases in his clothes. The young man hurriedly stood up too.

'Can I ask one more question?'

'What is it?'

'Do you have any advice on how to let go of what you have?'

'You sound like an old soul.'

Death awaits everyone. And in life, there are highs and there are slumps. If the young man had a strong materialistic greed, he wouldn't have quit his job to pursue his dreams.

But he was constantly fretting over what he should do if he didn't want to die with regrets, and because of that, as much as he was concerned about what he'd gain in the future, he thought a lot about what he might have to let go in return.

In one's younger days, it was harder to 'give up', but with passing time, the moment would come when it became harder instead to 'not give up'. In that sense, the young man thought his older self might be better positioned to give him advice on how to let go.

'Even at my age, it's still hard. It's a question we spend our entire lives finding our answer to.'

Although it wasn't a straightforward response, the young man nodded. And to the older man at the dark blue door, he said, like a farewell greeting:

'All the best for whatever you're focusing on now!'

The old man had not mentioned anything like that in their conversation. In fact, he wasn't doing much at all. Because he'd been very depressed recently. He turned back with a questioning look, and the young man smiled.

'Didn't you say you're what I make you? You're still too young to be letting go of everything in life.'

Was that supposed to be a joke? Suddenly, an image flashed from his dimming memories. Fifty years ago, when he'd looked at his older self, he'd never once thought of himself as a feeble, useless old man. The realisation hit a deep chord within him.

It was as if a small flame had rekindled in burnt firewood. In his heart remained the passion that was in his younger self. The elderly man gazed steadily at the young man.

'You've done well. Keep it up.'

Just as he opened the door, he turned around. 'If you have a chance to learn how to make spaghetti carbonara, do so.'

Thud. The blue door closed. In the shop, Bo-reum folded her arms and was needling Mun about time and space laws, her voice angry, but seeing the elderly man was back, she quickly rearranged her expression.

'How was it?' Mun smiled.

Unlike Bo-reum, he was calm and relaxed as usual.

'I kept wanting to tell him things I know I shouldn't. It was tough to hold myself back.'

What he had wanted to tell his younger self was the story about his wife. Today was the first anniversary of his wife's death.

It was a car accident that took her life. He wanted to tell his younger self that he'd meet a wise and bright woman, get married, have kids, and forty-nine years later . . . If she told him that she was going to the shops, do everything to stop her from getting on the bus; no – drive her there yourself.

However, he couldn't say anything. It felt as though, had he said anything, all the memories he had with his wife would vanish in that instant. It was pure chance that they'd met in the first place.

Like in a drama, it was a chance made possible by several coincidences one after another. Hence, he couldn't bring himself to tell the young man about her. He worried that if he said anything he shouldn't, it'd mess up the fragile thread that had brought them together.

'Because it's short, it's beautiful, isn't it?'

His wife had said that of life once when she was looking at a flower in the field.

'Our memories too. That's why I don't want to return to the past.'

That was her response when he told her how a magical encounter would one day give him the opportunity to speak with his younger self. He was always in awe of her wisdom. Hence, this time round, instead of following his own greed, he tried to do what she'd have done.

'Compared to her, there are so many ways I'm still lacking.'

Outside, it was still snowing. Mun served him a warm drink, and the old man wrapped his cold hands around the mug. On his left ring finger, the mark of the ring remained obvious.

'I thought I should offer some advice to the younger me, but it looks like I'm the one getting the advice.'

After his wife's passing, he had been spending his days listlessly. Losing his greatest pillar of support in life cut deep. All he had wanted was to join her as soon as possible.

'I thought it was too late to start doing something new at my age, and that it was time to put my affairs in order. It's such a foolish thought – to give up trying because I'm afraid. I think I should try something new. I want to stand proudly in front of my wife when I see her again.'

The younger him was always up for challenges. Because of that, he met his wonderful and beautiful wife who fell for his drive and passion.

Looking into that pair of passionate eyes of his younger self that she'd fallen for back then lit a warm spark in his heart.

'On the way here, I saw an ad for a theatre club, and they don't have any age restrictions. I think I'll apply.'

Thanks to the warm drink, the cold had receded slightly. He got up, ready to head out, and just as his hand touched the doorknob, he turned and smiled at Bo-reum.

'You were right. I learned a lot. Thank you so much.'

'Oh? Ah, thank you.'

Bo-reum was flustered. Why did the elderly man thank her instead of Mun? But she returned his smile.

'Goodbye then.'

Just as he exited the door, a memory flitted through his mind. In that vague recollection, the Moon Rabbit had looked different.

'Oh! You changed your hairstyle. Last time—'

He turned, only to see that the door had vanished. He had only taken a few steps, but the door chime had faded away and the dark brown door was nowhere in sight.

It was the same fifty years ago. Everything had vanished in an instant. And when he told people about it, everyone thought he was cracking a joke. He chuckled at the memory.

Even though the bell chime was gone, the reverberations seemed to linger within him.

Time to head back.

The snow was still falling, but just as he had when he arrived, he took a big stride forward.

'Ahh.'

The young man stirred awake. He was lying face down on the table. He remembered taking a ring and pushing open the yellow door, but now, in his fuzziness, he wondered if it'd all been a dream.

'How was it?'

A face loomed in his line of sight, and he jumped. He was still in the bar, and in front of him was the short-bobbed, bunny-eared woman who had served him the drink. Right now, she was scribbling furiously in her notebook.

'Spaghetti carbonara . . .'

The last words of the old man were still ringing in his ears. However, he had no idea that this was his future wife's favourite food, so he didn't take much notice and soon forgot about it.

'So how was it? The future you?' The woman repeated her question eagerly, her eyes shining.

'Ah. He seems to be living a better life than I imagined,'

the young man replied as he tried to make sense of the lingering feelings tugging at him. Her absurd words must've gotten to him. That was why he had that dream after he dozed off.

'I feel refreshed.'

He'd never thought it possible to feel that way after drinking alcohol. But the self-doubt, the anxiety that'd plagued him were wiped away. Instead, the passion that he had felt when he'd quit his factory job, and his resolve welled up to take their place. The heavy rain outside had also stopped.

'Hmm?'

His fingers brushed against a cold object. He picked it up. It was the same ring from his dream. He recognised the unique pattern.

That same pattern remained etched on his mind, which was why, years later, he chose the same-patterned ring to propose to his girlfriend.

'Aha! He's paying with this.'

Smiling, the Moon Rabbit picked up the ring. He felt his mood dampen, as though it was his own possession being taken away. But since it'd cover the cost of his drinks, he nodded. And technically, it wasn't *his* ring.

'You're really lucky. I bet you'll thank me in the future,' Bo-reum exclaimed happily, but that exuberance didn't reach the young man. He simply nodded and got up from his seat.

'Goodbye,' he said.

Just as he put his hand on the doorknob, the door opened. A man with green hair entered. He was wearing a severe look, so the young man averted his gaze and walked out.

'You're back?'

'You. This . . .'

Unlike the Moon Rabbit, who was grinning, the man's

brows furrowed deeper as he glanced at the empty glass on the table. His voice cut through the air, so that even when the door was closed, the young man could still hear him from outside.

'Didn't I tell you that it's illegal to mess with time? It might cause some unintended consequences in the future!'

'Oh, it's okay! There isn't a problem. I saw it.'

'How can you see something when it hasn't happened?!'

The young man felt a stab of guilt, as if it was his fault, and he quickly headed off.

Chapter 8
From Moon to Bo-reum

On the bookshelves arranged at exact intervals, the stories were snoring lightly. A delicate scent hung in the air, making it feel like taking a walk through a forest.

'This way.'

Mun weaved through the aisles, his expression relaxed. There wasn't a single label on the shelves, but as the ex-custodian, he could get around with his eyes closed.

'Can we hurry? What if we get caught?'

Bo-reum followed anxiously behind. The memory of the sirens ringing piercingly during their last visit sent shivers down her spine. She imagined the red and blue lightbulbs jumping out at her at any moment and catching them both in action.

'Wait. I'm looking for a book.'

Mun spoke as though they were browsing leisurely in a bookshop. However, in this library, they were neither customers nor visitors. They were thieves.

'Anyway, who wrote all these?' Bo-reum asked.

Remember the common saying that books are the doors to a different world, allowing you to indirectly live the life you've never experienced, stir sweet imaginations and dream of new frontiers? The books in the library weren't too different, only that instead of fictional stories, they were connected to real lives.

'People, of course.'

'Who?'

'Everyone.'

The bookshelves stretched on infinitely. Bo-reum's gaze swept across all the books pressed tight against one another, and her lips turned down as she frowned. Mun, who was watching her, gave a faint smile.

'You too.'

'Me? How do you know?'

'I've read it.'

Her eyes widened, but the next moment, she looked at him shrewdly. Smiling, he turned his attention back to the shelves. It was impossible to know what he was thinking.

'Did you finish reading it?'

'I did.'

'Really? So how did it end?'

She could hear her heart pounding. He didn't look like he was joking. How would her life turn out? Would she, like Pamina, surmount all obstacles to achieve her dreams?

Pausing, he turned to face her. 'Want to know?'

Burning curiosity and the urge to cover her ears and flee tugged at her at the same time. She hated how her destiny seemed to hang on his words, yet she craved the knowledge. Bo-reum nodded.

'Tell me.'

Mun moved his lips. 'I won't. You didn't tell me, either.'

'Me? What do you mean?'

That didn't make any sense. She pressed him for an

explanation, but Mun simply pressed his lips tight and walked ahead. Bo-reum tilted her head a fraction. What happened to his usual mischievous self?

'You're lying, right? I've never written a book, and if I did, how can I write about the future?'

For a while, Mun remained silent. And when he spoke, there was a flicker of bitterness in his voice.

'Yeah, I lied. I have no idea – who wrote these books, where they came from, why they exist.'

Bo-reum blinked. Given his power to make those magical drinks, how could he be so clueless about his main ingredient – books? That was strange.

'These books exist, and my job was to take care of them. No one has any idea what to do with them, except to keep them safe and never to interfere with the stories within. At least that's what the celestial beings believe.'

The celestial beings. Until now, Bo-reum had no idea where exactly this 'sky' was. The earth she'd seen from the moon was beautiful. The blue waters, green vegetation, the people walking on the land. However, the sky that was seen from the earth wasn't visible from the universe. The atmosphere simply looked like cotton candy clouds. She couldn't see the libraries, their vast collections of books, the Tears Bunnies or the puppies who manufactured dimples. She was only here because of Mun's magical door.

Bo-reum turned to him. 'You're a celestial being too, right?'

Mun nodded. To her, he was an enigma. The longer she worked with him, the more questions she had. Just as she was about to give up trying to understand, as per usual, a book caught her attention.

'The books in this section are aggressive, be careful,' Mun warned.

'Aggressive?'

'If you touch them, you might be forced to read them.'

Mun's warning came just as Bo-reum's finger brushed against the book's spine.

A dark hand ripped out from her shadow, covered her mouth and dragged her down. Panicking, she willed her arms to transform, but as her muscles grew bigger, so did the hand.

'Ah—'

Bo-reum tried to scream but with the firm hand over her mouth, she could barely make even a muffled sound. Meanwhile, Mun had absent-mindedly walked on ahead.

Her eyes roved anxiously, desperate for something that might help. The book she touched opened its jaws wide like a monster.

'Ugggh!'

There was a flash of light from the book and the black shadow overpowered her completely. *TWACK!* The book snapped shut. The lights faded, and the book dropped limply to the ground. On the front cover were the letters: *FROM MOON TO MUN*.

The story goes like this.

In a world near yet somewhat far, libraries housing vast collections of books existed in the sky, each taken care of by a custodian.

'I hereby commend you for your contributions in maintaining the law and order of the heavens as the custodian of Library 527.'

Nobody knew how these books got there, who wrote

them, or where they came from. Every day, new ones, the numbers impossible to count, simply appeared, and as a result, the heavens needed more and more libraries, and of course, more and more custodians. Occasionally, the custodians gathered to exchange best practices and award medals to the top performers.

'Congratulations.'

Receiving the commendation on stage was a man, one of the most-skilled custodians and protector of books. Applause broke out, a mix of respect and jealousy, hearty congratulations and looks of envy.

Only the man receiving the prize remained expressionless. Beneath his dark green hair was a pair of sharp eyes.

It was Mun.

'It's been a long while. Shall we head out to celebrate?' the custodian from Library 500 suggested. Despite being a lot older than Mun, he looked much more spirited.

'I'm sorry. I need to get back to my library.'

'Hey, hey, you need to take it easy. You already have a bright future ahead. I heard you're going to be promoted to one of the first 300 libraries. That's amazing! How does it feel to be doing so well?'

'I'm just doing my job.'

'I've been a custodian my whole life. Never have I seen anyone else who has caught as many thieves.'

'Thank you.'

To the man's friendly overtures, Mun only returned clipped answers. With a snap of his fingers, a portal to the library appeared. Mun gripped his plaque and stepped through the door.

Behind him, the man clicked his tongue. 'I also haven't met anyone so aloof.'

Mun ignored him. The door closed with a thud and vanished.

With heavy steps, he passed through the rows of shelves which were placed at exact intervals and sat down at his usual chair, tossing down the commendation plaque carelessly among the stacks of documents on the table.

Fatigue blurred his usually sharp gaze, and he closed his eyes. As he let out a sigh, his exhaustion broke through the dam, crashing upon him like waves.

Zero thefts. Ever since he became a custodian of Library 527, he had been maintaining the pristine, jaw-dropping record. The number of libraries and custodians might have increased, but each library still held its own enormous collection of books. If not for his ability to create doors that went anywhere, such a record would be impossible.

I'm tired.

He leaned his body against the backrest but found it hard to relax. Back then, he was proud of himself. It was as if he'd found his calling – something that only he could achieve. Where did that sense of fulfilment disappear to? It was all the fault of the thieves and their anguished cries.

If you can find your own book, you can change your future or your past.

An old rumour. Nobody knew if it was true, but the glimmer of hope it'd given to many also gave the custodians a lot of headaches.

Not Mun. Catching the thieves who stole books for their selfishness and greed was a breeze for him. He never found that to be a problem.

Until the day he caught that young man and everything changed. Mun was about to call in the guards as usual when the man prostrated himself in front of him, his forehead hitting the ground in a hard thud.

'Please, I beg you. My entire life, I haven't been a good son. Punish me all you want. But let me beg for forgiveness from my mother.'

Clutched tight in the man's hands was his own book. Mun gave a start.

How did he manage to find his own book in this vast space? And why did he wait until his mum was gone before he realised his mistakes? Perhaps it'd be okay to allow him a short conversation?

A mess of thoughts flitted through his mind, but before Mun could react, the guards arrived and dragged the man away.

The young man was only the start. Occasionally, Mun met others who also managed to find their own books.

'My daughter is sick. I'll gladly suffer the pain on her behalf. Help me.'

'Why me? What did I do wrong in life to deserve this?'

'I'm not asking for much. Just an average life, just let me live like the others.'

His heart ached at their despair, but there was only one thing he could do – shut out their anguished cries, close his eyes to their tear-stained faces. Follow the rules, crush his emotions.

If only those books didn't exist . . .

Then there wouldn't have been such futile hopes.

If there's a god that makes the world, surely it must be a mistake to create these books? Or do They like to watch people mired in misery like some perverse hobby?

Beep— beep— beep—

A red button hidden among the stacks of documents was flashing. A trespasser. It had been a tiring day, with the prize ceremony on top of everything else. All he wanted to do was take a break, leave the serious work for tomorrow, but it looked like he was being denied even a brief respite.

He sighed heavily, but the turn of the doorknob drowned out his frustrations. Mun rearranged his expression before stepping through the door. He needed to stay focused. No matter how devastated the intruder was, how they pleaded with him, he'd have to subdue them, take away the book and call for the guards.

If taking away a book is a crime, perhaps the custodian is the biggest criminal.

He ignored the seed of doubt within him. Stepping out, he parroted his usual lines. 'Please show your certificate of entry to the library. If you're trespassing . . .'

'Ah.'

Mid-sentence, he met the gaze of the intruder. Round eyes, mouth slightly agape. But unlike the others, there was no fear or anxiety in her eyes.

Oh?

And unlike the others who at most tried to take a couple of books, what she was doing was on a completely different scale.

What the hell?

A bookshelf had completely toppled. Like the aftermath of a disaster, the woman was on the floor, piles of books strewn around her. The book on top of her head slid down with a thud, revealing a short bob and long bunny ears.

'You aren't from here.'

Mun's brows tightened. Fatigue deepened below his sharp eyes. Clearly she was going to be a handful.

Where did she come from?

He'd better tread carefully. Who knew? There could be some complicated conflicts of interest that were beyond his knowledge. He wouldn't want to get an earful from his superiors. Irritation shot up in him. Meanwhile, the intruder, who was now sitting up on the ground, seemed to be slowly recovering from the shock.

'Here it is! My certificate of entry.'

She held out a piece of paper. True to her word, it was a certificate granting her access to the library. He couldn't believe it. Thus far, no other thieves had managed to produce a certificate.

'Hmm.'

His eyes combed the paper, and he let out a long sigh, as though things were as he expected. The validity period on the certificate was too ridiculous to be true. It was a counterfeit, a bad one too.

'How is it like to travel through time, eh?' Mun asked sarcastically.

If the certificate had expired, at least that would make some sense, but the validity period on the paper was a date in the far future. It was a top-notch forgery, and he'd almost fallen for it. Too bad they made a mistake on the most crucial line.

'Well, it's possible, isn't it?'

She nodded. When faced with her confidence, Mun was flustered. He looked at her personal details on the certificate.

Strong rabbit.

So, she was a guardian of the universe. His impression of them were that they were righteous and trustworthy, but it looked the same couldn't be said of all of them. Here was a dishonest rabbit who lied through her teeth.

'Please comply with our checks.'

'Why? I gave you the certificate.' She smiled brightly, a hint of mischief at the corner of her lips.

Mun's jaw tightened.

Do rabbits usually like to play stupid pranks like this?

How could she still smile? Mun was annoyed. This was a library, a haven for knowledge where silence was golden. Not a place for silly pranks.

'If you don't believe me, how about checking it with your counterfeit detector? You have one in your retreat, don't you?'

Mun's frown deepened. The audacity. Acting like she knew everything just because she came from the future, if that was even possible.

Every library housed a private space – a retreat – for the custodian, and most of the time, a counterfeit detector could be found there. Mun, too, had one in his retreat. Even though she acted like she was all-knowing, it wasn't that shocking. She'd probably made a wild guess.

'Forgery is a serious offence.'

'I told you! I didn't forge anything!'

Mun frowned. What blatant lies. Once he confirmed that the document was a fake, things would not end with a simple warning like the other cases of trespassing. His superiors would also have no choice but to escalate the matter. He wondered if she knew the seriousness of her actions to be behaving so confidently.

'Fine, check it then!' she challenged.

On any other day, he'd simply ignore her and call for the guards to take over the matter. However, he had had a tiring day, and his nerves were already stretched to breaking point. He'd teach her a lesson on the grave consequences of her lies.

'I'm giving you one last chance. Speak the truth.'

'This is the truth. I'd never lie to you.'

The woman didn't avert her gaze, and in her words was a deep resolve. It was impossible to know what she was thinking about. Sighing, he conjured a door back to his private space. As he twisted the doorknob, he turned around to offer a curt warning.

'Stay here. I'll be back.'

At his retreat, Mun moved past the documents stacked like stone pagodas and searched around the area. Finally, in a corner, he found the counterfeit detector – forgotten and sitting unused, looking like an antique.

Brushing away the thick layer of dust, he placed the certificate in the document tray and pressed a button. Like a fax machine, the paper was pulled in. All that was left to do was wait.

'I'm starving. Can I use your kitchen?'

Mun jumped. The woman had followed him into his retreat. It looked like she'd passed through the door before it disappeared.

'I told you to wait there,' he said, frowning.

'How can you leave me alone? What if I run away?'

His head throbbed. No matter how hard an intruder tried to escape, as long as they were in the library, he could easily catch them with his ability. Having her invade his retreat irked him more than anything else.

The retreat wasn't just a resting area for a short break. It was the only private space offered to the custodians, where they cooked and slept; a place where they could disconnect from their work. The woman was intruding into his personal space.

'Go—'

Just as he was about to yell at her, he was distracted by loud beeps from the machine. It looked like the old device had an error. He frowned, and while he wrestled with the machine, loud clanging filtered from the kitchen.

'Damn.'

He muttered under his breath. But luckily, in no time, the machine seemed to return to normal. As if right on cue, the thief came out of the kitchen. *Did she use some special power to jam the machine just now?* The timing was too good to be true, but it didn't make sense, so he shook his head. It was probably a series of coincidences.

'You happened to have all the ingredients I needed, and I also made fresh coffee.'

With a smile, she set down a tray on the table. A sweet aroma blended in perfectly with the rich fragrance of the coffee and it triggered his appetite.

'It should be quite delicious.'

Quite delicious? What an odd expression. Feeling annoyed, he couldn't help but nitpick on her words.

Be-beeeep

He grabbed the printed result. There it was. He'd chase her out the next second.

HUH?

He strode purposefully towards her, only for his aura to wilt by the time he reached the table.

Glancing up at him with a fork in her hand, she said, 'I didn't lie, did I?'

Mun checked the results slip several more times.

How could they make such a mistake?

After a moment's fluster, he concluded that it must've been

an error on the part of the employee who had issued the certificate. Those bureaucrats liked to act like they were above others, fastidious to the last detail. To think they couldn't even get the validity period right!

'Looks like the issuing authority made a mistake. Please go back and get it reissued.'

'You owe me an apology! You guys are the ones who made a mistake, yet you treat me like a criminal.'

'But you also have the responsibility to check for any mistakes in the document.'

'They told me everything was fine! That there wasn't a problem! Those liars.'

She puffed up her cheeks in annoyance, but it was clearly for show. She didn't look upset at all.

'. . . What a nuisance,' he muttered under his breath.

Just as he was about to firmly turn her away since the dates were invalid, she deflated her cheeks and smiled.

'If you're feeling sorry, then please join me and have some too. I used your kitchen and your ingredients, so let's call it quits. We're even.'

He didn't feel sorry at all. But perhaps the best way to get rid of her as soon as possible was to go along with her. Besides, he was also feeling a little peckish.

'Where did you come from?'

He handed her the visitor registration book. At least if he got her on record, he'd have something in his defence should anything go wrong in the future. It'd be the fault of the issuing authority who made the mistake with the dates, not his.

'I'm in charge of the moon. You can call me Moon Rabbit.'

She scribbled her name and signed. And she signalled towards the plates, inviting him to try her cooking.

'These are soufflé pancakes, a French dish made with whisked egg whites. Add the ingredients you want, pop it into the oven and it'll rise beautifully. A good soufflé is thick and jiggly, unlike the usual flat pancakes. Although I didn't use an oven for these.'

Was it because she was in charge of the moon? Even though she was from elsewhere, she appeared very well-versed in earthling food.

'I oiled the pan slightly and cooked the batter over a weak fire on low heat. Try it. It's like eating clouds.'

She helped herself to one of the pancakes and gobbled it up. And just as she had with the first one, she drizzled honey over the remaining two. Mun, who didn't have a sweet tooth, wasn't very keen, but the woman ate another one and pushed the remaining piece to him, so he had no choice but to pick up his fork.

Ugh. Sweet things are not my favourite.

He stuffed the entire pancake into his mouth, as if hoping to get it over and done with. Like eating cotton candy, the thick pancake began to dissolve in his mouth immediately, and he tasted a light hint of egg on his tongue. Even though there was a generous drizzle of honey, it wasn't as sweet as he had imagined.

'Uh.'

Suddenly, the landscape shifted. *Splash.* He fell into a sea of blue. It wasn't dark like the bottom of the ocean; all around was bright and clear. Neither did he feel breathless or scared.

Calmness surrounded him as if he were floating in mid-air. Just as the thought came to him, the surroundings morphed into the sky. The feeling of being submerged in water turned into the buoyancy of being in the air. Then he found himself falling. Or was he flying? The land and sky were inverted. He was rising but getting closer to the ground. At the edge of the sky, he could make out the greyish glow of buildings. The next moment, he was sucked into a dark brown ceiling.

'Hello.'

The voice coming out of his mouth wasn't his. The inverted world had righted itself again and he was sitting at a café. His voice shook, and opposite him, a woman was also visibly nervous.

'What's the important thing you wanted to tell me?'

She spoke carefully, and towards the end, her voice trailed off. She'd guessed what he was about to say.

They had known each other for only a month. He'd been coming up with excuses to meet her, and even though she knew that they were just excuses, she always agreed to meet.

They went out for meals together, spent their time idly at cafés. They didn't do anything special, simply keeping each other company as time passed them by, but to the man, they were the most heart-fluttering and loveliest moments in his life. So, he made up his mind.

'Er . . . I . . .'

He had prepared his speech, but he couldn't stop trembling as he fumbled with his pocket.

'I'd like you to have this.'

With difficulty, he pulled something out. It was a bracelet. Nothing expensive or fancy. When they walked past a street vendor, she had murmured that it was pretty. But in his palm now, it looked too plain. His resolve withered.

I should confess with something better next time.

Just as he hesitated, the woman grabbed his hand. He jerked his chin up. Her face blushed crimson but she didn't avert her eyes. A smile spread across her face like the colour on her cheeks.

'Thank you. I'll treasure it.'

She glowed with joy, as if what she'd received was not a plain bracelet but was covered in diamonds. Perhaps, to her, the feelings that the bracelet represented shone brighter than the most brilliant of gemstones.

It wasn't about shining trinkets but the warmth of a human she loved, and in the man in front of her, she could feel that affection emanating from his broad frame.

In the first place, perhaps a confession was not something to 'challenge' yourself to say aloud but a 'confirmation' of feelings. Their gazes met in a smile.

'Haa, haa—'

A delicate tremble reverberated in his heart. Between gasping breaths, Mun recognised his own voice again. His widened eyes narrowed sharply.

'What did you do to me!' he yelped.

There was an edge to his voice. Mun was usually calm and cool, but things were spiralling beyond his understanding.

'I asked you what you did to me!'

He slammed his fists on the table. The Moon Rabbit's ears perked in alarm. Anxiety hovered in her eyes.

'I was just cooking with the ingredients in your kitchen.'

A thought flitted into his mind, and he quickly headed to the kitchen. What was emanating residual heat wasn't a stove or an oven, but a book.

'That's fascinating.'

The Moon Rabbit slid up next to him. Stunned, Mun quickly jumped aside, embarrassment colouring his face. Try as he might, he couldn't come up with an excuse.

'How did you make the book light up?'

In the sky, it was forbidden to meddle with the books. That was why libraries and their celestial custodians existed. If a custodian himself broke the rules, he'd be axed immediately.

'That's illegal, right?' she asked innocently.

And seeing him fumble, she smiled.

'It's going to be a big issue if you're caught, right?'

I was too careless. What should I do now? Should I come up with an excuse? How much does she know about the books? Is she related to the higher-ups? Should I swear her to secrecy? Or should I confess?

The thoughts tumbled in his mind, with every imagined scenario ending badly. He couldn't help but come up with the most extreme situations.

'I'll keep it a secret. In return, let me stay here for a while,' she said.

Mun was stunned at her unexpected request. What was she secretly planning? Was she going to loot the library?

'I won't steal. But let me read all the books I want.'

'No way.'

His reply was sharp. Even with the certificate of entry, it didn't give her the right to read any book she wanted. And as the custodian, he wasn't supposed to, either.

What she was asking for was a blatant flouting of the rules. He'd rather get punished himself than allow anyone to use these books for their own gains.

'*Tsk.* But you read them.'

'I . . .'

He wanted to retort, but in the end, he kept his mouth shut. He pushed back his chair noisily and conjured a door. He'd send her away right now. Realising what he was up to, she quickly grabbed the table leg, which was fastened to the floor.

'Leave.'

'No. Just let me stay here. I'll keep quiet and not get in your way.'

Summoning all his strength, he tried prying her away from the table, but she refused to budge an inch. Her muscular limbs locked themselves around the table leg. She was indeed a strong rabbit. He snapped his fingers. The door opened and attempted to suck her in. The winds were so strong that it seemed as though the table was about to be ripped from the floor.

'W-wait! Mun! I read your book!'

He blinked. He had not told her his name. For a moment, he remained silent. Then he snapped his fingers once more and the door slammed shut. Patting down her messy flyaway strands, the Moon Rabbit steadied her breathing, and her muscular limbs returned to normal.

'My book?'

'Yes. I've read it.'

Everyone's stories were recorded and kept in a library. Mun had wondered if his own book, or maybe even books, existed somewhere out there. If so, how much was written? Was there an ending? And if his story was already decided, then what was the point of living life? What was waiting for him ahead? It was a chicken and egg question.

'If you let me stay here, I'll tell you a little each time. If I tell you everything now, I'm sure you'll chase me out right after.' She was still breathing heavily. Carefully, she shot him a glance.

Mun hesitated. There was no way of knowing if she was telling the truth. Even if she had really read something, it didn't seem right for him to know. Logic screamed at him to chase her away, but the frustration lodged itself in his throat. Eventually, he turned his head.

'Only for a short while, mind you.'

'Deal!'

She was in a cheery mood, as if oblivious to his anguish. If she had a tail, Mun knew she'd be wagging it furiously. And this was the start of their uncomfortable stay together.

Humming happily, the Moon Rabbit followed him everywhere like a puppy. However, the work at the library wasn't as exciting or magical as she had thought.

Soon, she got bored. Intruders didn't appear all the time, and a custodian wasn't a job that requires any travel. The number of books in Library 527 was fixed. Mun spent most of his time at his desk handling paperwork.

One day, when he didn't move an inch for six hours straight, she couldn't take it any more.

'It's been a week. Can't I have one book, just one?'

'No.'

Mun made it a point to stick to his routine even with her around.

'Isn't it boring? To be doing the same things all the time?' she grumbled.

'No.'

'And this isn't what you've been doing all this while, right? You're sticking to this routine just to chase me away.'

'No, it's always been like this.'

'That's a lie! You didn't touch the books at all!'

Mun rushed over to cover her mouth, but her voice echoed throughout the library. It wasn't as if there was someone listening in, but this was not something that should be shouted about. He glared at her, but she frowned back.

'Don't think I don't know anything! You've been reading the books every day!'

'How do you know?'

'I saw it in *your* book!'

He didn't have a retort for that. Did she really peek at his story? The past week had been terrible for Mun too. Exactly as she said, he had deliberately stopped his research because she was around.

'Just be your usual self! I told you I'll keep this a secret. We're in the same boat now, why are you being like this?'

'Bullshit. Who's in the same boat . . .?'

'Whatever, I don't care! Just do what you usually do! You want to read the books too, right? Just be yourself!'

The Moon Rabbit lay down on the floor and threw a tantrum. It didn't look like she would give in. The grind of a routine life had also blunted his sense of danger. Whatever. Mun was also feeling reckless. He went to his retreat.

'Okay, don't touch anything. Just stand in a corner.'

'All right, all right. I'll stay very still, as if I were dead.'

Placing a book down carefully, he murmured under his breath. His powers didn't stop at conjuring doors. With his voice alternating between a gentle murmur and an urgent whisper, the pages turned on their own and then stopped abruptly.

Heat rose from the opened book. He would try to recreate the soufflé pancakes.

'Here!'

Even though she promised to keep still, she helped with the cooking. He was going to chide her, but he held back. What was important now was to successfully recreate the dish.

After sifting the all-purpose flour into a bowl of egg yolks, he added a splash of milk, vanilla essence and sprinkled in some salt. The Moon Rabbit was tasked with making the meringue. Turning her arms more muscular, she added sugar to the egg whites and whisked. When it quickly reached stiff peaks, she slowly folded the whisked whites into the egg yolk mixture. They poured the batter into the oiled pan and watched it cook with the heat from the book. Soon, an irresistibly sweet aroma spread in the air.

'Looks delicious.'

He plated the soufflé pancakes, and following what she'd done the previous time, he drizzled some honey on top. They looked exactly like how she'd made them. Solemnly, he took up a fork, cut a small piece and put it into his mouth.

'. . .'

Silence. The Moon Rabbit, who had also taken a bite, laughed awkwardly.

'It's delicious.'

Mun didn't reply. Taste-wise, it wasn't much different from the one she had made. It was the same. However, this time, no vision intruded upon his mind.

He saw a flash of fragmented images, but they were so dim that he might have imagined them. It was a failure. What was in front of him were just normal pancakes.

What did we do differently from the previous time?

His fist tightened around the fork. Did she just get lucky before? He was so sure that he could recreate the experience. That since it had worked once, there was a possibility that it would succeed again, this time with a different book.

For a glorious moment, he'd thought that the answer to the riddle bugging him all this while would reveal itself. Sadly, it wasn't to be. It was like eagerly watching a balloon rising higher and higher, only for it to burst in the next moment.

'You're disappointed, right?'

'I thought you knew everything. Why are you even asking?'

'Haha . . .'

It was time to wake up from the dream. Time to face reality – the one he'd been trying so hard to avoid.

'You don't quite remember what you read, do you?'

That was when he realised.

Inside a story, it might seem possible to change the past or the future, but the books in the libraries had a fatal weakness. They were like dreams – at the end of one, you only remember fragments. All that's left are the lingering feelings. Even if you managed to change something somehow, you wouldn't remember what or how things changed, or worse, if something had changed in the first place. Seeing the past or future was nothing more than scattered memories that were of no help.

It's all for naught.

That was why he tried to make food using the power of the books. To make the vague, indistinct stories readable, and to make them possible to remember.

In his work as the custodian, he'd met countless people with regrets, heard their despair and suffering. But when he handed them over to the guards, he couldn't bear to tell them the truth – that even if they'd managed to find and read their own book, instead of being able to change something, they would not even remember much of it. He didn't want to extinguish what little hope they had. Instead, he wanted to help make their wishes come true.

But despite his efforts, he failed each time. When the Moon Rabbit made the soufflé pancakes, he had thought it was finally some sort of a breakthrough. But the truth was disappointing.

Or maybe in his heart, he'd already known that it was simply by chance that she'd managed to infuse the story into the pancakes. That was why he had subconsciously avoided the books in the past week. He didn't want to face reality.

Mun didn't want to experience again the disappointment of losing hope in the blink of an eye, like seeing a shooting star, only for it to disappear. He'd had enough. He was exhausted.

Perhaps it is best to simply leave the books on the shelves.

He had believed that the books must have appeared for a reason. An opinion that differed from that of his superiors began to take root in his heart. The books were meant to be read. He was now convinced. But just as how nobody could figure out how the books appeared, the books themselves were impossible to figure out, too.

'You should go back.'

Something broke in his voice. Mun slowly got up and headed for the library. The Moon Rabbit watched him walk away. She continued to stay in her seat and stared down at the pancakes.

Suddenly, a possibility flitted into her mind.

'Have you heard?'

It was the custodian from Library 500. He had an errand to run nearby and decided to drop in for a visit. He sat up straighter, his voice animated.

'Seems like a book thief ended his own life. He probably

thought having his own book would solve all his issues. Of course, in the end it was just a mirage. To think that there are still fools who believe in those rumours, what a joke.'

The mockery boomeranged and hit Mun full force in the face. Was he any different? He nodded vacantly.

'You're as boring as ever. All you do is work. Why not come to the party with me this time?'

'Thank you, but I'll have to decline.'

At Mun's stiff tone, the custodian of Library 500 made a sound of disgruntlement. Patting him on the shoulder, he got up and left. For a while, Mun stared at his vacant seat.

Just a mirage.

The man's words had left a bad taste in his mouth.

'Mun! I did it!'

It'd been three days since that failed attempt. Since then, Mun had holed up in the library and worked like a robot. In those three days, he had grown gaunt and listless.

'I'm telling you, I figured it out! How to make the stories compatible with food! I tried to confirm it—'

He cut her off mid-sentence. 'You're still here? I thought I told you to leave.'

'Ah. Anyway, it's the food—'

'I'm not interested.'

'Huh?'

The enthusiasm on her face dissipated. She tried to push up the corners of her lips.

'Mun, hear me out. I really got it figured out.'

Gingerly, she walked up to him. In her hands was a bowl of small cookies.

'This—'

'I said I don't care.'

Crash. The bowl was knocked out of her hands. At the clinking of the broken shards, her ears tensed up She quickly bent down, hoping to save the cookies, but he pushed her roughly away.

'Just because you read my book, do you think you know everything about me? What you remember is just fragments!'

He raised his foot and crushed the cookies. *Crunch.* The Moon Rabbit's face fell. Her red eyes were tinged with sadness.

'Leave.'

He should've done this sooner. Hopefully this would be the last he'd see of her. It was time to end the foolishness of being stirred by a flicker of hope. He was much more comfortable being alone. He knew better than anyone else how to be alone.

'Stop acting like a fool,' Mun spat out and turned away, leaving the Moon Rabbit with tears flowing down her face. He heard hurried footsteps behind him and a firm grip held his shoulder. He turned around only to hear a loud slap cut through the air. Lights exploded in his vision.

'Stop it!' the Moon Rabbit screamed.

Mun's cheek stung. He turned and saw a trembling hand. If she'd used her muscles, she wouldn't be feeling a tingling sensation in her palm as she did now. It looked like he hadn't been harsh enough. He looked down at the ruined cookies on the floor.

He snarled. 'These cookies—'

'I said, stop it! Don't throw away your dreams like this. Don't try to trick me. And stop lying to yourself!' the Moon Rabbit yelled.

The look of scorn froze on his face. Even though tears were brimming in her eyes, she refused to avert her gaze.

'Why are you giving up? Because you keep failing? Do you have no other choice?'

He was upset. Upset at the Moon Rabbit, who acted like she knew everything, upset at himself for being more affected than he should, upset at how frustrated he was, as though in his heart, he knew she was right.

'What do you know?'

'I know! Do you know how many times I read your story, over and over again? You're always like this. Talking about efficiency, simplicity and insisting you're right . . . You only see things your way, and then you give up when things don't work out!'

The words tumbled out of her in a rush, like her emotions were bursting through a dam. They'd only known each other for a week, but she was crying as though she'd held on to the sorrow for a long time.

'Your feelings, your dreams, they're important. Stop going on about *the best*, *the most* like a robot. And don't push me away. If you're having a hard time, say so. If you're happy, smile. Showing your feelings is not a weakness.'

As he watched her trembling lips, redder than her eyes, an unfamiliar emotion welled up in him. She was pointing out his weakness, to which, for the longest time, he'd turned a blind eye.

'Everyone needs a little help occasionally. It's like in those stories. Sometimes we need a pair of glass shoes, or like in that Korean folktale, a toad to help block the hole in the *hangari* jar.'

The Moon Rabbit's face scrunched up with sadness as she hung her head low.

'Let me help you. I have your back. In fairy tales, miracles also happen in the most desperate of times, right? When you feel as though your hard work has led to nothing, when the road ahead seems dark. If you can get past it, I'm sure there's a happy ending waiting ahead. You can't stop in the middle of a story.'

A moment of silence fell between them. Mun tried to think of a retort laden with hard, cruel facts.

'. . .'

But for some reason, he couldn't say anything. The Moon Rabbit was wiping her tear-stained cheeks with her sleeves and walking away. He remained on the spot. Just then, something crunched beneath his feet. He looked down. Carefully, he bent down, picked up a small piece of cookie and bit into it.

Whoosh—

A tiny flutter tickled his heart. But only for a moment. A puff of smoke, then it disappeared. The cookies were a failure. A bitterness spread in his mouth.

The retreat was the only space in the library that belonged wholly to the custodian. However, when Mun stepped inside, he could now find traces of her everywhere. He walked past the books whose spines were cracked open and sat down on the chair at his worktable. He usually spent as much time here as he did in the library, but it felt like it'd been a long time since he sat down alone.

What is it that I wanted to do?

Mun closed his eyes and sank into thought. What he was doing felt awkward and laughable, like trying to dig for treasure in an old musty room. He thought about why he wanted to be a custodian in the first place. It was an odd mix of wanting to fulfil his childhood dream of catching villains, and the attractiveness of a job coveted by many. Perhaps this was the root of his problems. The intruders he caught weren't the villains he imagined them to be.

People with regrets, those who'd lost their loved ones, those who got into unfortunate accidents. Their desperate pleas gnawed at him. If only their misfortunes could be wiped away from their books as they hoped. And if he, an outsider, thought this way, what about those people themselves? That was why he set out to do something about the books.

Despite his resolve, he couldn't do anything at all. It was impossible to remember the contents of the book, never mind make any changes to the story. Meanwhile, time continued to flow. He tried experimenting with various methods, hoping to find a suitable vessel for the stories. After several trials and errors, he discovered that it was possible to infuse stories into food, and since then, he'd been trying to find the right ingredients.

Meanwhile, all he could do was pass the intruders over to the guards. They cried and begged, but keeping his own emotions at bay wasn't as difficult as the first time. Over and over again, he acted as though he couldn't hear them. Indifference was much easier than empathy.

What's the point of carrying on?

When the custodian of Library 500 told him about the thief who ended his life despite finding his own book, Mun wondered if there was any meaning in what he was trying to do. It was a futile effort. Worthless. That was why he wanted to give up.

'Miracles happen in the most desperate of times . . . You can't just stop in the middle of a story.'

The Moon Rabbit's words rang in his ears.

So what if there's a miracle? What's going to change?

Life would still go on as usual. He'd continue to catch these intruders, hand them over to the guards and let nobody finish the story in their books. That was his job.

'Your feelings, your dreams, are important.'

Mun recalled how the Moon Rabbit had shouted through her tears, her feelings clearly etched on her face.

Feelings. Feelings. Feelings. Mun mulled over the word. Suddenly, a thought struck him, as though someone was whispering it in his ears.

Perhaps, all along, all I wanted to do was change my own story.

He'd believed that he was acting out of pity for those who'd cried and begged, as though he was a sage, a saviour. But that wasn't true. Instead of wanting to comfort them, he was hoping to receive comfort.

Slowly, he turned his head. Next to the crumbs on the table was a book that looked worse for wear. Clearly, the Moon Rabbit was the culprit. Despite knowing that she wouldn't remember the story, that she could only grasp at the vague feelings within, she had read it over and over again.

He glanced at the title of the book. *The Boy Who Sees.* He flipped to the first page and started reading.

'Ugh.'

He closed the book, trying to grapple with the awful nausea welling in him. It was the kind of story that'd bring a frown to anyone's face.

Just how many times did she subject herself to this?

He couldn't understand. Reading it multiple times could

still leave her with only feelings of discomfort. What drove her to stomach these emotions and keep going?

'I know! Do you know how many times I kept reading your story, over and over again?'

Mun thought about what the Moon Rabbit had said. Would his book evoke the same feelings? He thought of how he was always trying to push away anyone who tried to approach him. Perhaps his book would be no different. At that thought, Mun flipped back to page one again.

'Ugh.'

Reading it a second time didn't help. He still didn't remember any of the details, just the unpleasant taste souring his mouth. So, he started from page one again. And again. One more time. Gradually, the pain in the story sharpened, becoming more vivid. After he closed the book, some of the scenes lingered in his mind. So, he returned to the beginning again.

He saw the indulgent smile of the mother, the young boy awash in tears staring at her funeral portrait. He put himself in the scenes of the blind boy playing the piano. The boy grew up to be a young man. Mun journeyed with him as he enjoyed short-lived success before he went down the wrong path and lost everything. And when he finally realised it, there was no one next to him any more.

'Ack.'

Mun lost track of how many times he'd read the story. In the end, he could no longer take it, and he retched over the sink. But that didn't stop him from reaching again for the book. Over and over again, he read it, and finally, he understood. It was a book that was horrific until the very end.

That's right! The compatibility between food and stories!

Now he realised why the cookies the Moon Rabbit had made were so bitter. However, that wasn't enough. The cookies were still too sweet to hold the sorrows of the book.

What else? What else is there?

He rummaged through his shelves, not quite knowing what he was looking for. What was the food that people craved when they were sad? An ingredient compatible with misery? Wild ginseng? It was bitter but the heat was too intense. What else is bitter?

Perhaps some kind of juice . . .

Must it be food? How about drinks? Americano – no, espresso. And suddenly his eyes landed on the bottle of alcohol that he used to get rid of meat odours when cooking.

People drink it to soothe their sorrows; at the same time they drink to celebrate moments of happiness.

Alcohol. It fit perfectly. Before the bitterness on the tip of his tongue disappeared, he quickly sprang into action.

It wasn't hard to find the ingredients. With his powers, everything was just a door away. The hardest part was the measurements to get the flavours right. For a while, he spent his time travelling far and wide to learn how to make cocktails.

A month passed. He was so focused on his task that he neglected his custodian work. With the sparkling water he made from water boiled with the book's heat, he mixed in different proportions of spirits to make cocktails. In the clear glass, the layers of liquid shimmered like a rainbow. He picked up the glass, held it close to his nose and inhaled the fragrance. Then he tilted it carefully and his throat moved as he gulped it down.

'Ughhh.'

It was a success. However, the joy didn't last long. The pain and despair came rushing in. The crux of the story that he'd missed.

All this while, his focus was on trying to fuse the stories into food – the ingredients, the method of cooking. He hadn't been paying attention to the story, nor did he lend a true listening ear. But now, it was different. Instead of judging how it made him feel, he learned to feel for the protagonist, to genuinely hope to help him. If not for the Moon Rabbit, he wouldn't have been able to come to this realisation. He put the glass with the drink into a case and prepared to go out. He wanted to thank her properly.

'Moon Rabbit.'

He closed his eyes and thought of her. Her long bunny ears, her short bob, her bright smile, the tears on her face, her cherry-red lips, the words she spoke, her mood. And in front of him, a door appeared. A door that would lead him to her. He pushed open the door and stepped through.

'Mun!'

Her eyes rounded at the sight of him. She was in handcuffs, and next to her were two guards. It looked like she was on her way to attend a trial. Her lips moved, as if wanting to make an excuse.

'Erm. This. I mean, I can explain. There was a situation, you know what I mean, right?'

She must've done something reckless and got caught.

It'd been some time since he last went into the library, so he had no idea what was going on. But that wasn't important.

'There's a story I want to help. A young boy who got into

an accident, lost his sight, and later he made the wrong choices and lost everything. Help me.'

'Huh?'

'I want to change the story.'

The two guards, who were already shocked at Mun's sudden appearance, blanched at his words. They knew Mun. They knew that he was a top-notch custodian. They were there when he got the commendation plaque. A model custodian wanting to change the contents of a book? They stared at each other, at a loss for what to do. But the Moon Rabbit's face broke into a wide grin.

'Are you sure? It's going to be completely different from the work you've been doing up till now.'

'But if I can't change my day, how dare I dream of changing the contents of the book?'

Delighted, she broke away from the guards and ran towards him. Of course, to her, the handcuffs were as easily broken as if they were a toy.

'You took your time! Any later, and I wouldn't have been able to go with you.'

Leaving behind the stunned guards who were sweating bricks, the two of them disappeared through the door.

After this incident, Mun was quietly stripped of his role and privileges as a library custodian. But for once in his life, he couldn't care less.

The two of them were a good match, and in no time they fell into a routine of bickering over the smallest things. In other words, they became quite close.

Mun also discovered the meaning behind the Moon Rabbit's favourite phrase – *it should be quite delicious* – when she served the food. 'Quite' has the meaning of being more than the average. Not too much more, but just enough. And she rather liked that expression.

'What will happen will happen. What's the point of working so hard?' Mun grumbled, his cynicism rearing up again.

Unlike Mun, the Moon Rabbit was calm. 'Even so, how you feel about it does makes a difference.'

'That's just brainwashing yourself to accept your lot in life.'

'But there are also things in life that you won't want to change.'

To be able to read a story and to change it were completely different things. They continued to fail in their experiments. If it had been Mun alone, he'd have given up. But luckily, there was the Moon Rabbit next to him.

'But you should know that this isn't enough!' Mun exclaimed.

'Mun, you're too riled up. And if you're trying to make me upset, you're doing a great job.'

She knew exactly how to puncture his agitation. He sank down into a chair, and when he spoke, he kept his voice calm.

'Is there something you remember from my book that you hope won't change?'

'Hmm, hmmmmmm.'

With a cheeky snort, she flashed a sly smile. When she had that expression on her face, Mun could never quite tell if she was being serious or playful.

'Of course.'

'What is it?'

'That we'll enjoy running a shop together.'

'A shop?'

She held out a proposal. The writing was sloppy, but one thing was clear. She wanted to set up a shop that sold stories.

'That was a lie, right? About seeing this in my book?'

'Hmmm.'

'No way.'

The risks involved were obvious.

'Why not? Let's just do it!'

She attempted to bulldoze her way through his logic, but neither would budge.

Of course, in the end, it was the Moon Rabbit who got her way. When she lay on the floor to protest, he could only raise a white flag and surrender to her whims.

'I have told you several times now. Messing with timelines is highly illegal. You never know what the consequences will be!' Mun warned.

Infusing the stories into the drinks wasn't as easy as he'd imagined. Sometimes they got unexpected results.

Once, the Moon Rabbit was happily mixing several samples that Mun had made, and somehow they ended up with a drink that'd allow the person to meet their future self. Even though this meant a possibility of changing the story, it was risky, so he warned the Moon Rabbit several times not to touch it.

'Oh, it won't be a problem. I saw it!'

'How can you see what will happen in the future?'

Despite his warnings, she went ahead to serve the drink to a young man. If Mun had been there, he'd have put a stop to it, but of all the times, the customer came in when he was away.

'In this world, nothing *simply happens*. There must be a reason why we managed to make that drink. I believe it's for the young man who just stepped in,' the Moon Rabbit had said confidently.

'What makes you so sure?'

'The moment I picked it up, he walked in.'

'That's nonsense.'

Even though the Moon Rabbit had a habit of getting into trouble, this time, Mun was really angry. She tried to explain herself, but Mun went into his room and slammed the door shut. Shocked, her bunny ears flopped sadly.

'Huu—' Mun sighed. In his tiny room, he was leafing through a book on space laws. It was full of difficult words – 'time warp', 'theory of relativity' and what not – and it was making his head spin.

He heard a knock at his door, but he didn't turn around.

'Are you still angry?'

'Yeah.'

Even though he said so, the feelings had ebbed. It was more of a matter of principle. After all, the complexities of time were beyond his comprehension, so the anger that rose up quickly dissipated.

The Moon Rabbit approached softly and sat down next to him.

'Do you know why I left the moon?' the Moon Rabbit suddenly asked. Mun kept quiet, but even though his eyes remained fixed on the pages of the book he was reading, he was listening to her intently.

'In the past, people used to make wishes to the moon. Sometimes I tried to help them, but there were times I made things worse. I started to think that perhaps I wasn't meant to help them; they had the power to solve their own issues.'

This was the first time Mun heard her talking about it. He gazed up, and in between the curtain of hair, her cherry-red lips moved in a murmur.

'I stopped trying to help. And as time went by, fewer people made wishes to the moon. This made me oddly disappointed, because it meant people had stopped looking up at the night sky.'

These days, whether it was in the day or at night, people rarely looked up to the sky. Perhaps they were able to solve their own issues, or maybe there was simply too much on their minds to even think of what was above them.

'I thought if the moon was prettier, perhaps they might remember us. My childhood dream was to become a designer of the stars, just like the fairies. That was why I decided to leave the moon. I wanted to search for materials.'

Their eyes met and the Moon Rabbit smiled. She looked a little more adult-like than usual.

'The young man often gazed upwards into the night. So, I gave him the drink. It feels like I was meant to do so. Like destiny.'

'A beautiful excuse.' Even though he was being sarcastic, his expression softened. He wasn't angry anymore, whether for real or in principle. 'But you should've gone sourcing materials to decorate the moon. Why come to the library?'

Mun had intended it to be a light-hearted question. But just as the earth and moon had different gravity, his question weighed more heavily on the Moon Rabbit.

With her bunny ears standing erect, she fell into deep thought. Instead of answering, she asked another question of her own.

'You know what they say about life being a path with a

destination? But don't you think that life feels more like the running track in a big stadium?'

'What do you mean?'

'If it's a path, it means that as long as we keep moving forward, we're getting closer to the destination. If we do the things we enjoy, life's going to get happier, and if we meet something sad, we're going to be mired in misery. But that's not how it truly is. In life, there are ups and downs, sadness and happiness. It's like the earth and moon. Or the earth and sun. Revolving around each other.'

While Mun didn't quite get the analogy, it was a fresh perspective. He leaned back in his the chair and mulled over her words. He closed his eyes, imagining himself running on the track in a big stadium.

'But it's so meaningless.'

'What do you mean?'

'Nothing ever changes. Even if you keep going at full speed, it's not as if you'll get anywhere. In the end, you're just going to exhaust yourself.'

'That's not true. You're not the only one in the stadium. There are those who've started running earlier, some who came later. But in that moment, it's like you're all in it together and you could encounter each of them at any point of your journey.'

In his imaginary track where he'd been alone, he added people.

'What's important is not the speed, but the company you keep.'

Mun opened his eyes, and their gazes met. Was he imagining things? There was a blush of colour on her cheeks as she nodded in earnest.

'Mun, do you remember the first time you ate the soufflé pancakes?'

He remembered the shock of having images intruding his mind, but because it'd been quite some time ago, he couldn't remember the exact conversation they depicted. He vaguely recalled the faces of a man and woman shyly sitting opposite each other at a café.

'What if instead of a confirmation, I want a challenge?'

She was referencing the story of the man and the woman, but Mun was too obtuse to see it. With her cheeks puffed up, the Moon Rabbit let out an exasperated sigh and held out something as if trying to change the mood.

'What's this?' Mun asked.

'Since we're opening a shop, we'll need name tags!'

Pinning the name tag that said *MUN* on his chest, she pointed at her own.

'Read it.'

'*Bo-reum.*'

Her sulky expression vanished, and the corners of her lips lifted.

'Only those who know about the shop will be able to read this as Moon and Bo-reum.'

'Then what about those who have no idea?'

'They'll see *MUN* and *MOON RABBIT*.'

And that was how the shop came to be.

And that is how the story of *From Moon to Mun* ends.

'Whoa!'

Bo-reum jerked awake, her limbs flailing noisily.

'You're awake?'

She slowly looked around her at a cosy space with several

tables. A warm orange glow slanting on the walls; the scent of an old bookshop. She was back at the shop.

'What happened?'

As she tried to gather her scattered memories, she checked her hands. She remembered following Mun to the library. Saw his book. And suddenly, a shadow hand had pounced on her, its grip stronger than her muscular arms.

It felt like I was sucked into a different dimension.

But she couldn't seem to recall what happened after that.

'Well, basically, you didn't listen to me and you got into trouble again.'

She remembered her fingertips brushing against the book at the same time he warned her against it. It was careless of her to do that. At least she could admit this. But was it really her fault? If he had warned her earlier, she'd have been more careful. Feeling wronged, she stuck out her bottom lip.

'What do you mean *again*? When did I get into trouble?'

Mun smiled. It was his usual mischievous look, but today, there was something different about it. Had he always looked this gentle? Something stirred in her hazy memory.

'I read your book.'

Mun, who was clearing the plates, paused his hands and slowly turned towards her. She was frowning, as if trying to piece together the fragments of her memories.

'You worked with a strong rabbit last time?'

'I did.'

'Your girlfriend?'

Something shook in his calm face. *Oho.* Curiosity piqued, Bo-reum was eager to know more.

'Why didn't you mention it? I'd love to know her.'

'We lost contact. She left.'

'Mm? As in the two of you broke up?'

She remembered asking him about farewells, and that time, his eyes had looked sad.

'Ah. I mean . . .' Thinking that she'd said something she shouldn't, Bo-reum's eyes darted around nervously. Because Mun was staring at her, she got even more flustered.

'Why did you break up?'

Don't ask!

Sirens wailed in her head, but curiosity got the better of her. Since she couldn't take back her question, she stared intently at his lips, as if waiting to hear a forbidden secret.

'She had to go back. There was nothing I could do.'

'That's nonsense. You should've tried to keep her by your side.'

'She came from a faraway time. That's like the other end of the running track.'

'What do you mean?'

'Well, she was just a friend who lived far away.'

'What? Then how did you two meet in the first place?'

She tagged behind Mun who headed towards the kitchen.

'By chance. Just like how earth came into existence. If there had been even the slightest difference, it would have been too hot or too cold for life. We happened to meet right then, like destiny.'

'That again? About chance becoming destiny?'

Mun answered with an affirmative smile. He was back to speaking in riddles.

'So it was a bittersweet farewell? Don't you think it was such a pity?'

'Of course.'

'Then you shouldn't have let her go!'

'Like I said, I had no choice.'

'That woman was too much! Are you sure she wasn't using you or anything like that?'

Mun, who was flipping something in a frying pan, broke out into peals of laughter. It was the first time she heard him laugh without inhibition; she was a little embarrassed.

'What's so funny?'

'Maybe you're right.'

Then you should be angry. Why are you even laughing?!

'What did she say before she left?'

That we'll meet again.

The tear-stained face in his memory overlapped with the Moon Rabbit's look of indifference. A perfect overlap.

'It's ready.'

A soufflé pancake cooked without an oven. Bo-reum's gaze followed the three thick and delicious-looking pancakes that Mun was plating. The curiosity swirling in her head just moments ago vanished.

'What's this?'

'Try it. It should be quite delicious.'

Just say it's delicious. What's with that odd phrasing?

Captivated by the delicious smell, she decided not to nit-pick on his choice of words.

'Wow, amazing.'

The scent filled her mouth as she took a big bite. Soft and round, the pancake resembled a full moon. She ate one, Mun took one, and as they were eyeing the last pancake, the door opened with a tinkle.

'Welcome to the Moon Glow Bookshop.'

Smoothing the creases in her clothes, Bo-reum hurriedly

took a menu and went to greet the customer. By now, she was able to grab the menu without waiting for Mun, taking whichever caught her eye.

Because what was important wasn't the menu but her bright smile.

The Hidden Story

Tinkle—

Mun looked up and froze.

'Are you closed for the day?'

The woman looked cautiously around, like a scared cat. Her clothes, especially her hat, which was pulled low, were shabby. Mun stared.

Perhaps feeling the pressure of his gaze, the woman shifted her shoulders uncomfortably.

'If you're closed . . .'

'No, please come in.'

His lips moved, but they were unnaturally stiff. The appearance of the woman stirred up memories of someone who'd left a long time ago.

It wasn't a lookalike; she was Bo-reum.

'Ah, okay.'

The woman wondered if it might be wiser to leave, considering his odd attitude, but she complied and sat down in a corner of the shop. She planned to drink to her heart's content, and she didn't want to be among busy crowds, so this was the perfect spot.

'Enjoy.'

Instead of a story cocktail, Mun served her a normal

alcoholic drink. Because today, he wanted to listen to her story.

'Kyaaaa—' She made a sound of satisfaction as she knocked back the liquor as if it was plain water. In fact, most people wouldn't even gulp down water that quickly. In no time, a red flush appeared on her cheeks.

'Assholes. Horrible humans! Don't give me that crap about *That's how society works*. Freeze to death, y'all!'

Her hat dropped onto the ground, and her bunny ears flopped as she slumped forward on the table.

'I worked so damn hard!'

Awash with tears, the woman continued to complain, saying that she came from the moon, that she wanted to be a designer of the stars – what any other person would dismiss as drunken gibberish.

That was when he realised. This was not the Moon Rabbit he knew. Or rather, this was her younger self, before she had met Mun.

The timelines must've crossed. The Moon Rabbit from the future returned to the time she came from. While Mun continued to carry the memories they'd shared, this Moon Rabbit had no idea who Mun was.

'You're always coming and going as you please,' he muttered softly.

Too soft for the drunk woman to hear him.

'There's so much I want to tell you. How can you be so good at lying? Every single time. So, it wasn't because you read my book that you knew me, right?'

The drunk woman remained oblivious to his grumbling. In any case, she had enough on her plate as it was.

He paused. And after a long silence, he muttered, 'I'll give in. I always do.'

'I'm really hardworking, I can do anything . . .'

Right now, they were in the same space, talking at the same time, but they were speaking over each other. To get to her, first he'd have to dust off the weariness in her heart.

'I believe you.' He spoke in a bright, clear voice befitting a bartender. She looked up. 'That you came from the moon, and that you're a strong rabbit.'

And that you're amazing.

The name tag that he'd kept for a long time, the tag that she'd gifted him, found its way back to its owner.

'Would you like to work here?'

Her long bunny ears bobbed along as she nodded vigorously. 'Yes! I'm a good worker. Leave all the physical work to me.'

From that moment, they were on the same track in the stadium.

Author's Note

'It's amazing that you can whip up those magical concoctions,' the Moon Rabbit once told Mun in awe. However, Mun begs to differ.

Whether it's the cocktail that allows you to meet your future self, a drink that calms you down, or even magic, Mun doesn't think that any of these are special. If someone asks him, he'll tell them that what's truly amazing is the ability to lend a listening ear, offer words of comfort when a friend is having a hard time.

What's special is a parent's love, passion for your dreams, discovering what happiness means to you, and forging your own path regardless of what others say.

Just like how we wish there was magic in the world, Mun wants to hear our stories and he's rooting for us.

Thank you for being a part of this moment.

'We're always ready to welcome you with a smile. Welcome to *The Moon Glow Bookshop*, where chance becomes destiny.'

Translator's Note

There's something to learn in every story, but only we can change our own.

I knew right from the start that I'd love this novel, not just because it's about two of my favourite things – books and cocktails. What an intriguing idea it is, that a story can be infused into a drink, allowing us to savour and to experience it with our senses.

The Moon Glow Bookshop is full of magic and wonder, but it doesn't offer an easy solution, and I love it. There isn't a cure-it-all potion to help us forget or to solve our problems. The real power here is the ability to listen, whether it's to others or to our own hearts.

It's said that one can only find their way to the *Moon Glow Bookshop* once in their lives. But you're special. You hold the story in your hands. Drop by anytime, and Mun and Bo-reum will always be here to welcome you.

It's been a privilege to 'live' in the *Moon Glow Bookshop* for months. Mun and Bo-reum are dear friends now (I love to hear them bicker) and know I'll be back for sure.

Shanna Tan
June 2025

P.S. I wrote this little note in my favourite cocktail bar in Bangkok. Mun and Bo-reum aren't here, but wherever we are, there are always stories to be told. We just have to listen.

Dongwon Seo was born in Seoul in 1993 and grew up in Incheon. He majored in mechanical engineering and is working in the IT industry. His debut novel, *The Moon Glow Bookshop* was released through crowdfunding and was an instant bestseller.

Shanna Tan is a literary translator working from Korean, Chinese and Japanese into English. Her translations include the bestselling *Welcome to the Hyunam-dong Bookshop* by Hwang Bo-reum. Born and raised in Singapore, she is currently spending some time in Bangkok.